Well, well, well this book makes for a rollercoaster of a ride. This book throws you around like washing in a tumble dryer. Throwing twist and turns at you until right at the very end. When the author is ready to lay out what has exactly been happening in this book and then boom everything makes sense. Wonderful.

- **Karen W**

A brilliantly twisted psychological thriller that kept me guessing right to the end. The plot was dark and complicated, yet easy to read. There were twists aplenty and secrets in abundance. The characters were well thought out and original, their background was revealed slowly, adding to the suspense. The descriptive writing transported me with ease to another country and culture. A really good read.

- **Sarah K**

I loved this book. The story was compelling and fairly easy to follow. The story although complex is enthralling and I didn't work out 'the whodunnit' until near the end. Definitely a good read. I will look out for more by this author.

- **Lenore S**

Ellie, Ellie, Ellie. What a ride. Behind Blue Eyes by Claire Duffy seductively draws you in and then tosses you around like a sock in a dryer. I loved how descriptive the setting was. It was easy to get completely lost in the twisted tale. I can't wait for the next in the series.

-**Rachelle S**

BEHIND BLUE EYES

CS DUFFY

1

What were the chances I'd meet the man of my dreams, fall absurdly, appallingly, head over heels — all that written-in-the-stars cheesy crap I'd spent a lifetime making puking faces at behind my friends' backs — pack up my life and move to Sweden, only to have him be eaten by a bear whilst having a slash in the woods?

I mean, knowing my luck, not out of the question.

The minute the ferry dropped us off on the tiny island on the farthest reaches of Stockholm's archipelago, Johan had announced he was off for a pee and the thick forrest that began just beyond the little rocky beach behind me appeared to have eaten him whole. I glanced at my phone, but as I hadn't checked the time when he disappeared, it did nothing to confirm whether he had been gone for two minutes, or ten or twenty.

It had been at least ten minutes, I was sure. Maybe closer to twenty. No, probably five, at most.

I'm really shit at judging time.

A huge sky awned over the worn, sun-bleached jetty where I sat; bright and clear and unbroken by so much as a single cloud. The air smelt fresh and pure, with a slight tinge of sweetness from the pine forests that seemed to cover every island I could see. The water was so crystal clear that I could see pinky-grey pebbles twinkling in the sun several feet below the surface. It was all flawless and pristine and empty. *We ain't in Wandsworth any more, Toto.*

Other than the faint ripple of the Baltic Sea lapping gently against the beach, the silence was so deep it was almost palpable. I found myself half-wishing for the screeches of my mum's next door neighbours through the cardboard terraced house walls, fighting to the death over *that slag from the pub, I saw you fucking looking at her, I fucking did*; for the sharp whine of a police siren roaring up East Hill, the yells and grunts of some drunken idiots having a punch up in the road.

He couldn't have got lost, could he? The thatch of ever-green trees was impenetrable, shadowy despite the glaring sun. No, he knew where he was. He had made this trip dozens of times. We were on our way to his friend Krister's family's cottage — Johan had been coming out here since he was a kid. He knew the area like the back of his hand.

Maybe that was it.

He'd said Krister was coming to pick us up. Perhaps there was a road just out of sight beyond the trees and they ran into each other and — and what? They'd have come to get me. Or did they decide to swing by the cottage first, leaving me sitting here by myself? Surely not.

There he was.

I let go of a breath that was a bit pathetically shaky, and grinned as I watched him jog across the rocks towards the jetty. Good god he was gorgeous. Relief mingled with the familiar rush of affection, lust, and disbelief that this Viking sex god was mine as I waved and he stuck his tongue out at me.

He leapt onto the jetty and it shuddered under his weight. He was, there was no two ways about it, huge. One metre ninety-five, he had specified when I drunkenly slurred wonder at his height back on the beach in Thailand where we met. I don't have the first clue about the metric system, but took his word for it that meant tall. Broad shoulders, legs that meant he'd never known a moment's comfort on a plane, hands so enormous a glimpse of them could make a girl come over all unnecessary at the most opportune moments.

The first time I'd seen his hair loose around his shoulders, the morning after we met, I'd gone into fits of giggles. With his floaty blond mane, he looked like the sort of guy you'd see strutting about the cover of a romance novel and I'd asked him if his loins were heaving. He'd looked down at his loins in confusion and I'd laughed till I got the hiccups.

We met at the Full Moon Party in Koh Panghan. After moping around for a few weeks over a breakup that was more disappointing in its crapness than anything approaching heartbreaking, I'd got bored of myself and booked a solo holiday in a dazzling display of independence and girl power. Despite somewhat dreading it, it turned out to be utterly brilliant and I was just making up my mind to commit fully to a glorious life as a spinster of undecided age, when I staggered away from the main party to catch my breath and maybe stop the world spinning a tiny bit, and I tripped, literally, over the love of my life.

He was stretched out on the sand — in fact, I'm almost certain I remember trying to go around him but not appreciating quite how long his legs went on for. He was shirtless and his abs were so sculpted that you could grate cheese on them, and I heard myself asking if I could headbutt them like a goat. Somehow, this turned into a three week fuck-fest that resulted in some nasty sand burns and, six months later, a one way ticket to Stockholm.

What can I say, I'm a classy bird.

Can I just say I'm making this out to sound like it's nothing but lust, but it goes without saying that Johan is also the most amazing person I've ever met. He is kind and funny, even if his sense of humour is so dry that for the first few days I thought he was a bit of an arsehole. He's considerate and he listens and he's one of the only men I've ever met to think my job is genuinely cool — I'm a freelance investigative reporter and bloody proud of it — as opposed to finding it sort of interesting to begin with but sooner or later it comes out they'd prefer I was something a bit sweeter and less threatening. It's amazing how *I've seen more dead bodies than you have* doesn't really reel them in on Tinder, but go figure. Their loss.

I suppose I just focus on the looks thing because, to be blunt, he is so totally out my league that it blows my mind a bit. Not that I'm massively insecure or anything, I'm just — normal. My face is my face and it does me fine. It even verges on pretty in a decent light and with a good bit of slap copied painstakingly from a YouTube tutorial. It's just that I don't exactly get stopped in the street by model scouts, if you know what I mean. Even though, once upon a time my friends and I wasted weekends upon weekends hanging about Soho, posing like utter wankers, hoping to get spotted and not have to finish our GCSEs.

Still though, Johan didn't seem to have noticed. He flopped down behind me, draped his long legs on either side of mine, and wrapped his arms around my waist. I shifted a bit, because I was wearing a vintage steal that was my absolute pride and joy, a psychedelic, flowery sixties sundress that I'd leapt upon on Portobello Road with a whoop of joy years back. I adored it, but it was made from some bizarre synthetic fabric that has probably since been outlawed. If I sweated even the teensiest bit whilst wearing it, I instantly smelt like a cow that had been dead for about a week. Brushing my hair was out the question lest static electricity set me on fire.

'Krister just texted,' Johan murmured. The feel of his stubble against my neck sent little shivers down my spine. 'He is on his way to pick us up, but he will be a few minutes late.'

I was mildly curious as to just how this mysterious Krister was going to pick us up, given there was nothing that remotely resembled a road in the vicinity. Presumably there was some kind of track or something just out of sight. I'd find out soon enough.

'That's good,' I said, leaning, back against Johan's chest with a yawn. 'The ferry was a bit late,' I added. 'I was afraid he would be waiting.'

'Why? You cannot control the ferry.'

I shrugged. Johan could be so literal sometimes. 'You know what I mean, it just wouldn't have been the best first impression.'

'Why would the failing of the ferry company affect his opinion of you?'

I elbowed him and he chuckled, nuzzled my neck. 'He will love you because I love you and because you are funny and amazing and beautiful.'

'Well that's alright then.' I reached up to stroke his cheek as he planted tiny kisses along my collarbone and I suddenly really wished we weren't spending the weekend in the company of strangers. Remind me again,' I said,

'Krister is the one you met on your first day of school, right?'

Johan nodded. 'Yes. I didn't know how to tie shoelaces, and the teacher ordered him to help me.'

'Wait, didn't you tell me you start school over here at seven?' I grinned. 'How did you make it to the age of seven without learning how to tie your shoes, you plank?'

I'm certain I imagined him flinch, just for an instant, before his easy smile returned.

'You are correct, I was an inadequate child.'

'Well you're perfect now,' I said firmly, just in case he thought I had been serious.

'And you met Liv and Mia in high school?'

'We went to the same elementary school also,' Johan replied, 'but Krister and I were terrified of girls until we were — well actually until we were about twenty-eight, but we were able to pretend by the time we were maybe sixteen or seventeen.'

'Is that when Mia and Krister got together?'

I knew most of this already, but I like to have all the information straight in my head before I meet new people. I'm not sure why. Nobody, to date, has given me a pop quiz on their lives and loves before deciding to be my friend, but best be prepared. Ideally I'd have chosen to meet his best friends for the first time prior to spending an entire weekend on a deserted island with them, but the couple of times we'd tried to get together over the past few weeks, it had always fallen through at the last moment.

'No they were just friends for years, then in our twenties they started to have sex sometimes, and eventually they become a couple.'

'And Liv doesn't have a boyfriend, does she?' I said.

Johan shook his head.

'Won't that be a bit shit for her, spending the weekend with two couples?'

Johan shrugged. He was shielding his eyes from the sun, scanning the horizon for something. 'There he is,' he grinned.

I followed his gaze and a dart of sheer terror shot through me. A tiny motorboat was ripping through the waves towards us. It wasn't Krister, I told myself. It couldn't be Krister.

When Johan announced we'd be getting the ferry out to Krister's family's summer cottage for the weekend, I'd pictured one of those gigantic ships that go between Dover and Calais. I'm still no great fan of them, but at least they're huge enough that I can normally find a spot out of sight of any window where I can pretend I'm not trapped on a lump of metal being tossed about on top of thousands of feet of dark water.

But the dinky little tin can that had been awaiting us at the quay in Stockholm was about a fiftieth the size of a proper ferry. It was like a ferry had been shrink wrapped. My knees had just about given way when I realised that Johan expected me to step foot on a death trap in the form of a sun-dried ferry.

'Can't we take that one?' I'd blurted desperately, pointing to the sort of enormous floating block of flats across the harbour that was more my cup of tea.

'No, because that one goes to Helsinki,' Johan had grinned, tugging my hand to pull me back into the queue to board. Icy chills were washing over me and I knew that there was only a deep yoga breath or two between me and puking in the face of the cheery kid checking tickets.

Somehow though, I'd survived. Even though the ferry shuddered like no one's business as it backed away from the quay, and again when it picked up speed upon clearing Stockholm's city limits. I'd closed my eyes and breathed, doing multiplication tables in my head to keep thoughts of a watery death at bay, pretending to doze against Johan's shoulder. I was just about to hit the seven times table for about the fortieth time when Johan whispered to wake up because we were at our stop.

The motorboat was now bearing straight for us at great speed, and the thought flashed through my mind that it would be ironic if I ended up being killed by a boat while on dry land. At the last second though, it veered sharply to the right, missing the jetty by about a foot as it reared up and sent a spray of freezing water over us.

'He's a fucking maniac with that thing,' Johan laughed delightedly, giving Krister the finger as he scrabbled to his feet.

Krister hopped from the boat and waded, dragging it by a rope to secure it to the jetty, as Johan greeted him with a stream of rapid Swedish. I pretended to be concentrating inordinately on putting my sandals on as I tried desperately to breathe through the hard lump of terror in my chest that was threatening to suffocate me. *I'll just say no,* I decided firmly. *They can't force me. They can go ahead and I'll just wait for the next ferry back to Stockholm. It'll be fine.* But even as I thought it, I remembered Johan saying there was only one service a day, and I was far from sure I'd even make it back on the ferry without Johan leading me by the hand. The words *rock* and *hard place* came to mind.

'I guess you are Ellie,' Krister was saying, and I belatedly realised he must have been staring at me for a while. So much for first impressions. I did my best to compose my features into something resembling a smile.

Krister was almost as tall as Johan, but dark. His poker-straight chestnut hair was cut in an odd cheekbone-length style that reminded me of some early 2000s boyband member. His eyes were almost black and gave nothing away as he coolly appraised me. Johan was tossing our bags onto the boat, causing it to lurch alarmingly each time.

'Lovely to meet you,' I muttered, finally managing to get to my feet. I held out my hand as though I were about to chair some kind of business meeting, and after a moment's hesitation, Krister shook it with the tiniest ghost of a smirk.

Somehow though, a moment later I found myself squished on the tiny bench at the back of Krister's boat. Johan tried to take my hand but I didn't want him to feel how sweaty it was, so I leaned my head against his shoulder with my hands in my lap and he slung his arm across the back of the bench. Krister heaved the boat into reverse, swivelling the steering wheel like a teenaged boy racer, and the boat juddered as though it were about to break apart at the seams.

'Hope you can swim,' grinned Johan as the water behind us churned up and lashed out at the jetty.

'No,' I muttered, but my voice was stolen by the wind as Krister floored the gas.

2

'*Glad midsommar!*' called a voice, and a woman who appeared to be a gazelle in human form came galloping gracefully down the steep path to the tiny rocky cove on the island where Krister had pulled up. Johan and Krister were pulling the boat clear from the water, while I stood, knee deep in the Baltic Sea, hoping that a spot of hypothermia might shock my legs into stopping trembling. The boat ride had been every bit as bad as I'd feared, though at least mercifully short and somehow I'd managed to avoid screaming out loud when Krister took a corner at such an angle that the three of us were thrown nearly horizontal.

The woman, presumably either Mia or Liv, flung her arms around Johan and I caught myself hoping she would turn out to be engaged-to-Krister-Mia. She was almost as tall as the boys and her tanned legs seemed to start somewhere around her armpits. I'd never felt more like a Womble in my life. Her pale, straw-coloured hair hung in a shimmering curtain almost to her waist, and she wore a white peasant-style dress that made her look like an ethereal wood nymph and would have made me look like I'd wandered out in my nightie.

'Ellie, I am so happy to finally meet you!' she called in a twinkly, sing-songy voice as she waded out to meet me. 'I am Mia!'

'Hi,' I grinned as she grabbed the bag I'd half-forgotten I was holding. Engaged Mia. Phew.

'Don't you hate the way Krister drives?' She rolled her eyes and tutted. 'I'm so sorry, I shout at him all the time for it and I made him promise he would behave. He's such an idiot.'

'It was fine,' I lied with a smile.

When we got to the beach I steadied myself against a rock to put my sandals back on, realising with a sinking heart that my beloved vintage frock was now garish and heavy next to her floaty number. Despite the horrors of the journey, half of me was tempted to announce I was just nipping back to Johan's to change.

We made our way up the path towards Krister's family's cottage, them all skipping easily with their eight-foot-long legs and athletic resting heart rates; me scurrying behind, clammy and breathless and wishing I hadn't skipped the last forty-odd spin classes I'd signed up for. At least they were all chattering in Swedish, which saved me from trying to make small talk whilst wheezing like my Nan in the final throes of emphysema.

When the path finally evened out a bit, I could see clean over to the other side of the island. A wide expanse of aqua water shimmered in the sun. Unlike behind us, where the next island was so close the shadows of its trees reached the beach of this one, in front there was only open sea.

'Is this the farthest edge of the archipelago?' I asked when I caught my breath.

'Yes,' said Krister. 'Next stop, Finland. We are close enough to Russia that the Americans were able to pick up radio signals from the Soviet Union during the Cold War.'

'Really?'

He nodded. 'They rented part of this island for a few years, the only time it has been occupied by anyone other than my family. My grandfather said he didn't care about Communism but was happy to have the money to build an indoor bathroom. Every time he used it he would whistle *Yankee Doodle Dandy.*'

I laughed, but Krister didn't smile, and my heart sank. 'It's fascinating,' I babbled as he continued to stare at me impassively. 'Spies hanging about in your back garden? How exciting. What were they doing?'

'Just listening, probably,' Krister shrugged. 'We don't really know. My grandfather said he sometimes heard them building something late at night when they first arrived, at the other end of the island.'

'Wow, what did they build? Like a secret bunker or something? I'd love to see it.'

'Me too,' he said. 'My father and his brothers searched for months when they left, and years later so did my cousins and I. We never found any sign of it. Maybe it doesn't exist. The whole thing may have been a decoy for their real base somewhere else.'

'Suppose that's the CIA for you,' I grinned. 'Rude.'

He blinked at me in surprise.

'Because they're spies. Secrets and stuff. Kind of their thing.'

'Yes.'

Abruptly, he turned away, leaving me to scuttle after them for the last little of the path. I looked over at Johan as we reached the garden, hoping to catch his eye, but he was deep in conversation with Mia.

The cottage was — not what I was expecting. When Johan had talked about his friend's private island, I suppose it conjured an image somewhat more luxurious than the rustic little red clapboard cottage in front of me now, nestled in a small clearing. Half of it was covered in some thick creeping vine, almost as though the forrest were trying to reclaim it, and the sun-dappled garden was overgrown with long grass and wildflowers. Except for a bright orange kayak lying round the side of the cottage, it looked as though it should be home to a family of kindly rabbits.

Just as I was envisioning Mummy Rabbit inside cooking, complete with wire-rimmed glasses and gingham apron, I noticed the odd, wooden Maypole-like thing set up in the middle of the garden. It was decorated with wildflowers and leaves, and I stared at it uncertainly, trying to shake the notion that it was a bit disconcertingly... pagan. Like if you danced around it anti-clockwise while whispering a spell you'd raise a centuries-dead witch, or something. Krister caught me looking and grinned that little smirk of his.

'That is the *midsommarstång*,' he said. 'We set it up at midsummer to celebrate how summertime fertilises the earth.'

I nodded slowly, not entirely sure how to respond to that, then frowned as I noticed something. The two circles at the top of the pole suddenly struck me as, not entirely — un-scro-tum-like. 'It's a cock,' I blurted, and Krister burst out laughing.

'Yes, more or less,' he said.

'Covered in flowers, shagging your garden. Well of course.'

'Welcome to Sweden,' Krister sad, cracking a grin finally.

It was then I noticed the picnic table set up at the far end of the garden. It was covered in a pristine white tablecloth and set formally with delicate china, fancy silverware and flower centrepieces. Johan stood next to the table chatting to Mia. She had put on a crown of flowers and birch leaves, which didn't do much to dislodge the impression I'd inadvertently signed up for a spot of witch-raising.

'Is this — sorry, is it someone's birthday?' I asked, my heart sinking as I took in the fancy table and frantically tried to remember if Johan had told me it was a celebration and I'd somehow forgotten.

Krister gave me a quizzical look. 'It is Midsummer,' he said.

'Oh, right,' I nodded, wondering what the longest day of the year had to do with the fancy-dancy table.

Another woman — Liv, presumably — emerged from the cottage, carrying a platter of smoked salmon. If I'd held out any hope of Johan's other female best friend looking a bit less supermodel-like, it was swiftly dashed. Liv's wavy, strawberry blonde hair bounced in tousled curls around her shoulders and she wore a cream, ankle-length sundress I can only describe as a sexy lace curtain.

'We were expecting you one hour ago,' she said, looking straight at me, and my heart leapt into my mouth.

'I'm so sorry, our journey was a nightmare,' I babbled, darting forward. 'I'm Ellie, by the way.'

'Liv,' she said shortly.

I'm sorry, I didn't actually realise it was a party — can I do anything to help?'

'No, it is all done now.'

'Right, I see. Sorry, again. Can I — carry something, maybe?'

'No,' she repeated, staring at me with pale blue eyes that

managed to be simultaneously expressionless and cold, and an iciness slithered through me.

Liv had probably been cooking all day, I told myself, as we all took our places at the table, and was stressed to the hilt. One year at Christmas, my mum broke three wine glasses in a tantrum when she forgot about the roast potatoes in the oven and they got burned to a crisp. She was mortified and we've wound her up about it every year since. A slightly abrupt greeting was nothing compared to that. It was forgotten, I told myself firmly, taking a deep gulp of the rosé Krister poured for me.

MIDSUMMER MAY NOT INVOLVE occult rituals, but there was a special meal, endless toasts with shots of snaps that just about singed the back of my throat off, plus singing and dancing around the Maypole-cock. It was all a bit baffling. At some point during the meal, Mia noticed how bamboozled I was and they all started explaining the traditions, translating the songs and... something about dancing like a frog that I never quite grasped.

It was all so absurdly Swedish it almost seemed unreal. Between the blondes and the wildflowers and the pickled fish, they might as well be belting out *Super Trouper* while juggling meatballs, and... putting together furniture. Naked.

Johan seemed different in company, I thought, watching him horsing around on the grass with Krister. In Thailand it was just us. The first couple of times he visited me in London I'd arranged get-togethers to introduce him to my friends, but he'd always been really quiet, self conscious about his English — even though it's pretty much flawless — and struggling to follow the conversation over the background noise of the pub. After the second or third round of awkwardness, I told people I just wanted him all to myself on our precious weekends together.

Being with his own mates brought out a whole other side to him. I was pleased to discover he wasn't always so shy in company, but it was a tiny bit disconcerting. A little flicker of uncertainty brushed over me, and I took a healthy gulp of my wine.

It must have been after midnight by then. Though it was far from full dark, a shadowy twilight had descended and Johan and Krister were indistinct shapes in the gloom. Johan was verging on messy-drunk — we all were, to be fair — red-faced and shouting. He and Krister seemed to be mock wrestling for reasons that presumably made sense to anyone who understood the Swedish conversation. I was feeling a bit conscious that I was sitting there like a leaden lump, so when Krister shouted something and they all burst out laughing, I did too.

'Oh do you understand?' said Liv, her eyes as wide. Someone had lit the tea lights scattered around the table, and in their eerie glow she looked like china doll in a horror film.

'No, I — I just — it looks funny,' I muttered lamely, biting back the urge to point out I hadn't understood anything in well over an hour and was starting to wish I'd brought a book with me.

'Ellie, I am so sorry, we are so rude,' smiled Mia, turning back to me. Her crown of flowers was slightly lopsided, but I didn't detect any slur in her voice. Maybe she'd been pacing herself better than the rest of us.

'Not at all,' I insisted. I noticed I'd sloshed a few drops of my rosé onto the white tablecloth, and tried unsuccessfully to dab it up with my napkin. 'I'm happy just to observe and learn.'

Liv got up to join the boys. She jumped onto Krister's back with a girlish squeal, and I found myself feeling slightly relieved it wasn't Johan's. Mia wasn't the least bit fussed. She shouted something in Swedish to them, raised her glass, and turned back to me again.

'This must all seem very strange to you.'

'It's different,' I shrugged. 'But so interesting. I've got so much to learn about my new life, but I suppose one day it will all just be second nature.'

'What do you mean?'

'Just that — well, next year I'll know about Midsummer. I've already learned that you have to take a number to queue for service in a shop.' I laughed, remembering how I'd gone to a little hardware shop near Johan's flat to buy a plug adapter on my first or second day and had stood there like a wally in front of the counter, getting more and more incensed as other customers kept strolling in front of me to be served. Finally I'd clicked that they had all taken little tickets and their numbers were being called. I'd meekly taken my own ticket and hoped I'd imagined the judgmental look the girl behind the counter gave me when my number was called. 'And that's just my first week. Eventually I imagine I'll forget how strange it all seemed to begin with.'

'Oh, do you think you will stay with Johan forever?' Mia asked, her head cocked slightly to one side. I felt my smile falter. I took a large gulp of wine.

'Well I mean — it's early days,' I stammered. 'But — well, I wouldn't be here if I didn't -- I mean, he's Johan. He's pretty amazing.'

She nodded slowly. 'Johan is one of my best friends, I love him to death — ' She trailed off, shrugged and toyed with her wine glass, the candlelight flickering over her troubled expression. A little knot of nerves took root in my stomach.

'I mean, of course you know —'

'Of course,' I said firmly, with no idea what she was talking about.

'I just hope he —'

'You and Krister — Johan was telling me you'd all been friends since school?'

If she was surprised by the abrupt change of subject, she didn't show it. 'Yes,' she smiled. 'We knew one another back then, but Krister and I didn't really become friends until university, where we studied on the same course. It was five years later when I looked at him one day and thought kissing him might be a good idea.'

'And now you're engaged. That's a really sweet story.'

'It's quite boring, really.'

Johan, Krister and Liv came back to the table then, laughing their heads off, and I tried to shake the cold feeling that had settled over me. Krister seemed to be explaining to Mia whatever the joke was in Swedish, but when Johan flung himself in the chair next to me and reached over to rub the back of my neck, I felt a sudden wave of claustrophobia. Krister started to pour another round of shots and I shoved my chair back.

'I'm just — just going to get some air, for a second,' I muttered, fully aware of the ridiculousness of what I was saying in the middle of a garden. No one seemed to notice. Johan was leaning across the table talking to to Liv, and Krister had started to hum one of the numerous drinking songs under his breath as he handed the glasses round.

I made my slightly unsteady way across the garden. The sky overhead was white, but the thick canopy of leaves shrouded the woods in darkness and just a few feet in I shivered. I turned to glance back at the table, telling myself I was being an idiot, telling myself I should just slip back and join them.

It looked as though my chair had been pushed farther away from the table, leaving their gang of four balanced once more. Johan was facing me. I felt like a voyeur, spying on him from the shadows, but I couldn't take my eyes off him. His chiseled cheekbones suddenly appeared harsh and distorted in the candlelight. I could only see the back of Liv's head, but as he raised his glass in her direction, he looked at her with such an unmistakeable air of intimacy that my stomach heaved and for a second I thought I was going to throw up. I turned and fled, icy dew trickling over my sandals as I marched over damp moss and bracken.

Without a clue where I was going I walked and walked, deeper into the woods, fully aware I was probably walking round in circles. If this were a London night gone a bit tits up, I'd have been hailing a taxi and slipping into the night, and the thought that there was no way off this tiny island sent panic churning in my guts.

I was famous for my disappearing act. One of my oldest mates once told me she genuinely worried that one day I would actually get kidnapped and no one would raise the alarm because they would assume I'd just taken off.

Finally, I emerged from the trees onto another rocky beach on the other side of the island and the sight that greeted me took my breath away. The sunrise sat brooding on the horizon, a furious blood red, turning the sky the deepest, purest shades of pinks and oranges I had ever seen. Scarlet and amber and cerise and ochre were reflected on the glass-like sea, making it look as though it were somehow peacefully on fire, silhouetting the pine trees on neighbouring islands in black.

It was spectacular.

I resolved to go back to the party and try again, to climb onto Johan's lap, do a quick couple of shots to catch up and ask him to teach me the song about doing housework. I'd even choke down a bit more herring if it helped. It was all fine.

It was all new. We were strangers. I was an awkward Midsummer virgin, intruding on a celebration that was clearly precious to them.

Mia hadn't really meant anything about Johan, she was just a bit pissed. Of course Johan and Liv had an air of intimacy for heaven's sake, they'd been friends since they were kids. And Krister couldn't possibly think I was a complete moron. He didn't even know me. He just had resting judgmental face.

I'd been out of step with things, which was totally natural, and it had left me feeling a bit oversensitive and wobbly, and more than a bit daft. I took a deep breath. It was just like I'd said to Mia: in years to come, we'd look back on our first Midsummer together and piss ourselves laughing about how tense and weird it was.

It was about then that I noticed I was staring at a human skeleton, tangled in the reeds at the edge of the water.

3

I know how I sound right now. I know you're writing me off as
delusional, but please just—

*Let's start from the beginning. Was there anything unusual
about his behaviour that morning?*

No. Absolutely not. It was all completely normal.

He didn't seem stressed or anxious?

Not at all.

What about over the previous few days?

Please, you need to understand that none of this — none of it
makes sense. Everything was fine. Normal, boring, lovely. Just
life.

No money worries, concerns about his job, nothing like that?

How many times do I have to say it? You've got it wrong. He's
not what you — it's not how it looks. You need to investigate, find
out what really —

What do you think might have happened?

I don't know.

So how could you be certain it wasn't how it looks?

It's not my job to figure these things out, I don't know how it
all works. But I know him, and I'm telling you that there's some-

thing not right. You have to investigate. You can't let them get away with it.

Let who get away with it?

I don't know!

Then how —

Someone. Someone did this to him. Please.

4

'When they told me about their plans for Midsummer I assumed that meant I was invited, but when I woke up on the Friday morning they were gone.' Cas, an Iranian PhD student, shrugged. 'I spent the weekend reading.'

The café where the newcomers to Sweden coffee morning was held was bright and airy with huge open windows, art crammed every which way on the back wall, and the chairs and tables were battered and mismatched, as though it had been all been furnished by a car boot sale. I'd hesitated by the counter when I'd got my coffee, wondering how to approach the noisy group who had taken over one corner, then firmly told myself to get a grip. When I joined them, Cas had been chatting about *Swedish for Immigrants* classes with a couple of young Polish women — Nadja and Krista, I thought — who were both breast feeding babies.

I had just introduced myself to a German viola player called Nadine, and Jacob, a computer engineer from Nigeria who had gone to university in London, when a woman with short spiky red hair and an impish grin arrived in a flurry of warmth and apologies for being late but it was because she dropped her phone in the bath and now she knew nothing about anything.

'G'day, how're you going!' she'd shouted, greeting everyone with hugs. 'New blood! I love it. I'm Maddie. Welcome!' She enveloped me in a huge hug and announced she was off to order enough cake to feed an army.

'That's nothing, I lived here for more than one year before any of Henrik's friends spoke to me,' Nadja laughed, and her baby mewled in protest. 'For months I sat silently at dinners and parties wondering if I had become invisible.'

Maddie wallowed a mouthful of carrot cake. 'Lena's friends are great,' she said, 'and I get on with them really well now, but the first time she took me to a party — I guess I didn't consciously think about the fact that I expected her to introduce me around until she didn't. She just kind of wandered off and started chatting to someone, and I was like... guess I'm on my own then. And it was fine, because I don't mind making a pest of myself and just barging into conversations. But you're right, bless their little anti-social bums.'

'They are lovely after a while,' added Krista, changing her baby from one boob to the other. 'A long while, but still.'

'In my country,' Jacob said, 'when a new person joins, whether it is a community or a social gathering, it is natural for us to welcome them in. We say *hello, who are you, this is us and this is what we are talking about.* But this is not natural to Swedes. It is as though their conversation is a moving train and while the new person may be welcome to join, it is their responsibility to jump on the train, it will not be slowed down to allow them on. It is not cruelty or rudeness, it is just what is normal.'

'Totally. This Liv you mentioned,' Maddie added,

pointing her fork at me. 'Bet you dollars to doughnuts one of these days it will be like the sun coming out from behind a cloud and she will be the loveliest person you ever met. Loads of Lena's friends, I honestly just figured they were mute or something, then all of a sudden then one day it was like *where have you been, you beauty?* It's like an initiation, I swear — in fact, I bet you that's it. I bet you they all got together and voted unanimously to ignore the new people for about six months to a year — and only if we were still around after that, they'd allow us into the inner sanctum of eye contact and smiling.'

I laughed. 'I'm not sure I can imagine that with Liv just yet,' I said. 'But I'll take your word for it.' I tried to smile but my breath caught in my throat suddenly and for a horrible moment I thought I might cry or scream or something. I hadn't told them the half of it. 'It was just a bit — new and weird,' I finished lamely.

'We've all been there,' Katja smiled.

'Long as Johan's behaving himself,' Maddie grinned, and I'm fairly sure I kept my smile steady.

I was feeling so much better. Clearly I'd completely overreacted to what sounded like a fairly standard first meeting of Swedes. Well, until I'd found a dead body, obviously, but that was just a random awful thing. Everything was fine; it was just early days.

The fact Johan and I had got into a fight the night before meant absolutely nothing.

I'd been in a weird, grouchy mood all day. He'd been really quiet and it had been freaking me out, for no reason. I suppose I've just never been a big fan of silences, which is hardly his fault. I had just about convinced myself to stop being so ridiculous when I made a cup of tea to calm down and accidentally put this disgusting substance in it called *filmmjölk.* It's basically runny yoghurt but comes in a carton pretty much identical to milk. Just a few weeks in and I'd already ruined untold cups of tea with the bastard gloop.

Johan looked up from unpacking the dishwasher and mildly asked me why I was putting *filmmjölk* in tea. I screamed and threw the carton at the wall where it spurted over the pristine white paint and I was so horrified that I turned on him, blaming him for his country's failure to clearly bloody fucking label yoghurt.

'It says *filmmjölk* on the carton,' he'd said, baffled, and I stormed into the living room, so claustrophobic I could have torn off my own skin.

'I can't breathe, there needs to be another room.'

'I don't know why you are so angry.'

'Of course you don't. You have no clue. Everything is easy for you —'

'What is easy for me?'

'You have a job and a bank account and a library card — you can understand everything that's happening around you, you can talk to people —'

'What? People will speak English if you just ask them —'

But there was no stopping me. 'You know to pick your own salad when you order lunch and you only ever drink water so people don't think you're an alcoholic and you can find the onions —'

'Ellie, calm down, you are becoming —'

'Don't tell me to calm down.'

'Sorry,' he'd muttered, backing away. I paced his tiny living room like some rabid animal.

'Don't tell me what to think or feel or know. Just because you signed me into this country like some bloody library book does not give you the right to —'

'It was a government form, it means nothing.'

'That's not the point!'

'Ellie, please can you —'

'Stop saying please.'

'I didn't ask you to come here.'

He muttered the words under his breath, but they sliced through the air and pierced into me and suddenly I just wanted to sit down and cry. I stood there in the middle of the room, taking deep breaths to try to hold back the sobs, wondering if I should just pack my bags, get a hotel, book a flight to London.

'Why can't you find the onions?'

'What?'

'You said you can't find onions.'

His voice was so sweet, so pleading, that I felt a flicker of a smile tug at me. 'They're in a separate section, around the corner from the other vegetables. Where I come from, they are smack dab in the middle of the vegetables.'

He reached out, brushed my fringe from my face and I took a deep, shaky breath.

'That is where they should be.'

'Yes it is.'

'Well we will fix that. I will call the king tomorrow morning.'

I half laughed, half sobbed, and he stepped forward, wrapped his arms around me and I sank into him.

'I don't want you to be anywhere but here,' he whispered into my hair.

'He is behaving himself, right?' Maddie asked again lightly, with a kind smile.

'If someone was a cake virgin in this place, what should they order first?' I blurted.

'Oh the crazy caramel-marshmallow-brownie thing,'

Maddie said. 'It'll make your teeth fall right out your head, but you'll be so happy you won't care.'

I pushed my chair back and headed up to the counter.

'Hey, I'm going to give you my number.'

Maddie was suddenly behind me. 'It's a head fuck, the whole settling in business,' she said, her eyes searching mine. I nodded, taking the note she held out. 'Especially when you're one of us love refugees, you're dealing with all the intense shit of suddenly moving in with someone after it being long distance, and you don't even have your own mates around to let off steam to.' She gestured towards the lively group around the table. 'That's what this little gang is about. Use us.'

5

It hadn't taken me long to figure out that the island where Johan lived, Södermalm, was where the cool kids hung out. He was quite comically self conscious about it, swearing blind that he had lived there since long before the famous actors and vegans with funny hats moved in.

The day after I arrived, he'd taken the day off work and we'd gone for a massive walk so he could show me around. The whole place basically looked like the set of an art house film. The streets were wide and open, bordered by tenement-style blocks of flats in earthy tones of terracotta and mustard and olive, broken up by trees and well tended patches of grass. Pavement cafés were filled with ridiculously gorgeous people enjoying the sunshine, effortlessly stylish behind gigantic sunglasses. They were sipping crisp white wines, waving to friends who cycled by on gleaming black bikes with flowers and freshly baked bread in their baskets. It had struck me then that my days of nipping to the corner shop for a pint of milk in my well worn giraffe onesie were well over.

After wandering for hours, we'd ended up at the other end

of Södermalm. We'd bought ice creams from a van and sat down in the grass next to a little beach, and I'd prayed that I wouldn't end up with mine mostly all over my face as I normally did. I watched little kids splashing about in the water, kayakers paddling past, teenagers barbecuing on disposable grills, and Johan told me about the history of the island. His family have lived there forever, since it was known as *kniv Söder* because of all the knife gangs. Once upon a time Stockholmers from the main city were warned never to venture south of Slussen, the lock that connects Söder to the rest of the city.

'The actress Greta Garbo lived just over there,' Johan said, gesturing vaguely though some trees. 'And every biography of her describes how she grew up in the slums of Stockholm. My father and grandfather worked in a button factory on Hornsgatan —'

I burst out laughing. He'd been painting a picture of urban deprivation and violence, then button factory made it sound so charming and picturesque, as though things might be tough but Tiny Tim would still save Christmas.

'Yeah okay, but they were hard buttons,' Johan grinned. 'Tough buttons. Military buttons. In case we need to invade Russia.' The idea of the Swedish army invading Russia with their ghetto buttons from knife-Söder had us both in stitches, and then we started snogging and some teenagers yelled at us to get a room.

Johan's flat was just around the corner from the café, but I could never bloody remember the code to open the front door of the apartment building so stood on the doorstep for several minutes, staring at the keypad in frustration. He hadn't got around to getting a key cut for me, so we passed his set between us, with whoever was most likely to get home first taking possession.

Just as I was about to admit defeat and text him, the door opened and I grabbed for it. Two people came out, a man and a woman, both in dark coloured suits. The woman was about my age, dark, with huge almond-shaped eyes that hinted at a Middle Eastern background and the man older, something of the fading rockstar about him. His suit was crumpled, and his dirty blond hair streaked liberally with grey.

I held the door open for them to pass, but it wasn't until I had stepped into the lobby and was waiting for the creaky old concertina-doored lift that I clicked. They were detectives.

They'd come to the island that night, when Krister finally managed to get some service and dial 999 or what-ever the Swedish equivalent was. I had given my statement to a younger officer in uniform, just a basic description of how I had come across the body, but the two plain clothed detectives had interviewed the others. I'd only been a few feet away when they talked to Johan. I'd tried to catch his eye over the woman's shoulder, to send him a silent message of support, but he didn't see me.

That would be it, I thought now, as the ancient lift cranked and grunted its way up to the top floor. He'd been tired and freaked out and frustrated at not being able to help. They were probably just following up to check some detail or other.

In the flat, Johan was was sitting slumped on the couch, staring in to space.

'You okay?' I asked, sitting on the couch next to him.

He glanced at me in surprise, as though just noticing I'd got home, even though I'd shouted to him as I kicked my shoes off.

'Why would I not be okay?' He turned properly to look at me with an expression I couldn't quite read.

'I just saw the police in the hallway.'

He nodded slowly. 'Oh yes.'

'For heaven's sake, Johan, what did they want?' My voice came out sharper than I intended.

'Nothing,' he said finally, with a shrug.

'Just to check some details?'

He nodded. 'About the last time we were at the cottage. Last summer.'

'I don't know why they're bothering you with it, surely it could have washed up from anywhere. Can't they tell by, I don't know, the tides or something?'

He shrugged again. 'I don't know how they work.'

'Yeah, well, I suppose they are just doing their jobs.'

'I suppose they are.'

'It'll be nice when we can put it all behind us,' I said, pulling his arm around me and snuggling into his chest. 'I'm going to get my arse in gear tomorrow and start hustling contacts for some freelance gigs. I've been given a couple of names of British journalists based here to chat to, though apparently it'll be a bit tricky until my number-thingy arrives —'

'Personnummer,' he said quietly.

'Right, yeah. But anyway, no reason not to make a start on introducing myself around anyway. I'll rustle something up sooner or later, I always do.'

I felt him nod above my head. After a moment I realised he wasn't going to say anything more, so I reached over him to grab the remote. We watched TV in silence for the rest of the evening.

He absolutely was not having an affair.

 Then who do you think this woman was?

 Somebody from his work, maybe? An old friend? A friend of his sister's? She could be anyone. I have no idea.

 It would be helpful if —

 It would be helpful if you could trust the fact that I knew him better than anyone. I know it's not fashionable any more, believing in true love and soulmates and one being in two bodies. We're all supposed to be so independent, so cold and practical about the person we share our lives with. Like choosing a partner for a science project at school. Who is the cleverest, who will do their fair share of the homework, what marks they got on their last three projects. Then we complain that there is no love, no wonder, no obsession. But it wasn't like that for us. We were — we were more than that — He was not cheating.

 You came to us to tell us about this woman.

 Because maybe she knows something. Maybe she is the key to — if you could track her down, talk to her, get her to tell you —

 Tell us what?

 Tell you who killed him.

7

'Of course I'm fine, it was just one of those mad things.'
I took a sip of my coffee and put the vintage tea cup back on the little table. I could feel my mum's worry radiate silently from my phone. I was sitting at an outdoor table in front of a coffee shop near Johan's flat. I'd ended up there most days since I'd arrived, eeking out a coffee as long as I could whilst people watching the beautiful people.

There was a gorgeous little square with a fountain opposite the coffee shop. Every other time I'd been here, the grass was liberally strewn with what looked like off-duty supermodels, reading and having picnics and blethering into phones. There was normally a succession of toddlers making kamikaze breaks for the fountain. Despite their skill at terrifying their parents, these were no ordinary toddlers. They wore tweed trousers with braces and flat caps, ghetto chic onesies in seventies prints, paisley gypsy dresses. Until I moved to Stockholm, I never thought I'd find myself thinking *ooh I'd love that outfit, except for the nappy.*

Today though, it was pouring. Proper cats and dogs, the

rain a thick sheet bouncing off the pavement. I'd brought my coffee to my usual table outdoors under the canopy anyway. The streets were deserted and the window behind me steamed up, cutting me off from the bustling chatter of the coffee shop.

'How can you be okay?' Mum said I heard the tense note of fear in her voice and I bristled. 'A dead body! It must have been terrifying.'

'It was more like a skeleton, to be honest,' I said, just to be an arsehole.

I could hear the series of muffled thuds that signalled Mum was cleaning the kitchen. I could just picture her phone in the little sparkly holder she'd picked up at a discount shop on Lavender Hill, propped on the formica counter I've been on at her to update for years, as she dried dishes.

'The police reckoned it was most likely a wild swimmer or ice skater,' I added, though it occurred to me as I did that it hadn't been the police who suggested that — Krister maybe? I had started to point out that wetsuits don't decompose, certainly not so completely, then bit my tongue. What was the point? They were all in such shock. I remembered hearing Liv's short, choked sobs and I wanted to tell her to try to breathe deeply, but I couldn't quite get my mouth to form the words. 'I suppose they'll know more when they've done whatever tests they can do,' I said to Mum. 'It's awful, though. Absolute tragedy.'

'How horrible for you, love, when you've just arrived and everything.'

I heard a crash. She was either dumping dishes in the sink, or maybe putting plates back on the high shelf she can't quite reach.

'I'm fine,' I said, a bit too shortly. 'It was hardly my first crime scene. It wasn't even necessarily a crime scene. It's never exactly pleasant, but —'

'You weren't at work though, were you. It must have been a shock.'

'I suppose,' I muttered. I picked at the spicy cardamon bun I'd ordered but didn't really have any appetite for. 'I did have a bit of a wobble,' I admitted reluctantly. 'After I screamed and they all came running, we just stood there in a sort of huddle. Krister went off to find some mobile service to call the police, but none of the rest of us could move.'

That wasn't entirely true. I'd not moved. I'd stood on the beach, exactly where I had been when I first saw it, and out of the corner of my eye I could see Johan, Liv and Mia huddled together behind me. The scraps of grey flesh that clung to the skeleton here and there weren't the most appetising of sights; I supposed they hadn't wanted to come any closer.

'Anyway, Krister came back, and after a few minutes we heard the siren of the police speed boat approaching. My knees just gave way.'

'You never were fond of boats,' Mum said, and I grinned.

'It was the oddest feeling. One minute standing up and the next — not.'

'Must've been a bit romantic at least, collapsing into Johan's arms?'

My chuckle caught in my throat and I was glad Mum couldn't see my face. It absolutely wasn't his fault. He had no way of knowing I was about to do a dying swan act, and Liv had just burst into tears. 'It was actually one of his friends that caught me,' I forced a grin. 'Mia. Good thing the women are built to last here.'

'Oh well that's nice,' said Mum, and I heard her close the

cabinet doors. She'd start ironing next I predicted, and was rewarded with the squeak of the ironing board being opened. 'You know what I always say, love, boys come and go but it's your mates that catch you when you fall.'

I nodded. 'Yeah, maybe it'll bond us.'

'Mia, that's Johan's friend's girlfriend, isn't it? Is she nice?'

I thought of Mia wading into the sea to greet me, making an effort to talk to me long after Johan appeared to have forgotten I existed. 'Yeah, she's lovely. The other one's a bit of a wet blanket, to be honest.'

'She might shy.'

'That's not really an excuse for rudeness,' I muttered.

'No, of course not, it's just —' Mum hesitated, and I steeled myself. 'You know you can always pop back any time,' she said, her voice laced with hope. I was her only child and she'd nearly done her nut in when I'd wanted to go to university in Leeds once upon a time. In the end, I'd decided to stay in London anyway so I'd be available for work experience on the big national papers, but she'd not been any more subtle about her horror when I announced I was moving to Sweden to be with Johan.

Can't he move here?

He's got work.

You've got work.

I'm a journalist. I'm at work wherever my laptop is.

But how can you write for Swedish papers? You don't speak Swedish.

Mum, there's this thing called the internet —

I know, I just worry, love.

I know you do.

'Listen, I've got to go. Johan will be waiting, he's taking me to watch his team play football tonight.'

'Oh you'll enjoy that,' Mum laughed, and the tension

was broken. My aversion to football was well known. I'd even gone through a phase in my mid-twenties of announcing that forthwith I would exclusively shag rugby boys, but every one I'd met turned out to be a bit of a Hooray Henry which I couldn't be doing with either.

'Have a lovely time then, darling, and don't forget I'm only ever a phone call away.'

After we hung up I finished my coffee and mourned the waste of the cardamom bun, which I'd picked into a sticky mess. I stared blankly at the rain for a few more minutes, then got up, and found myself face-to-face with Liv, who was about to enter the coffee shop.

'Hi,' I said, automatically reaching out to give her a hug. She sort of leaned limply into me, and I stepped back. 'How are you?'

'Yes, I am okay,' she muttered, glancing over my shoulder into the coffee shop.

'I mean — with, everything. Neither Johan nor I could sleep the first few nights, it was so —'

'Yes, he told me.'

I flinched somewhere deep inside, as though someone had poked at my guts with a very fine needle. When had Johan told Liv anything?

'Right, well. Managed a couple of hours last night, finally, which was good.'

'Yes.'

'Johan is taking me to see Hammarby tonight. Not really one for football, but whatever makes him happy I suppose.'

'Hammar-bai,' she corrected, which sounded to me more or less exactly what I'd said.

'Thanks. Wouldn't want to get it wrong there and have the crowds turn on me.'

She smiled, the sort of pained, forced polite smile you give a guy who has just told a sexist joke but could fire you if you told him where to go.

'Okay. See you.'

8

The T-bana that trundled its way beneath the city was jam-packed. It seemed that Johan's team were playing their arch rivals from the other side of Stockholm, and both sets of fans were squished together in one subway carriage. The atmosphere was heavy with a sort of muted aggression, and there was so much testosterone in the air that I was slightly afraid if I breathed in too deeply I might grow a beard.

'Whatever happened to metrosexual Swedish new men?' I said, as a giant ginger dude, his hair and beard actually plaited like a Viking, stared me down for reasons best known to himself. Johan was holding on to the handle overhead and I held on to him, as he leaned down to whisper a detailed history of his football club and a translation of their anthem in my ear.

'It's a really beautiful song,' he was saying. 'When you hear everyone sing it together, it is just amazing. You know we started the tradition of fans singing in Sweden, we brought it over from England.'

'Dunno if it's a such brilliant idea to copy behaviour

from English football fans,' I said, making a face, and Johan grinned.

'English games are fantastic. One day, we will make the European league and —'

'You know in the anthem, why is it *just* today I am strong'?' I asked with a sly grin and Johan chuckled. 'Why don't you want to sing about being strong every day?'

'Because every other day they are shit,' said a gruff voice behind me.

I couldn't quite turn to see who had spoken because the ginger Viking had me pinned to Johan, but I saw Johan's jaw clench as he glared at the guy.

'Well that's just the height of wit.' I rolled my eyes, rubbing Johan's waist, or at least as much as I could without accidentally also feeling up the ginger Viking. 'And actually I was just pissing about, I think it's a really lovely sentiment.'

I felt Johan's every muscle clench as he spat something in Swedish, and the guy roared something back. The ginger Viking was shouting, possibly trying to tell them both to calm the fuck down, and I tried to get hold of Johan's hand, my other hand on his chest, as my heart leapt into my mouth.

'Hey,' I shouted over the rabble. 'Johan — he's not worth it — just leave it —'

I sensed Johan draw back and for an instant I felt relief, then he lunged forward and headbutted the guy over my head. I screamed. Bone and cartilage shattered with a sickening crunch, blood splattered my cheek, fists flew and the air filled with roars.

An arm reached over me and yanked Johan by the scruff of the neck, knocking him into me. I started to fall and Johan yelled — then suddenly I was yanked backwards, as

the ginger Viking shoved me into a corner out of harm's way
—

'No, I need to — he'll listen to me — Johan!'

Johan grabbed a guy— stocky, but at least a head shorter
than him — and rammed him against the door, punched his
already bloodied face —

From somewhere a siren sounded — the train jerked to
a stop and the doors opened.

Shouting and screaming, the crowd pushed their way
onto the platform and I was left alone, clutching onto a seat
back, trembling.

Twenty minutes later, I stood next to a map of the T-
bana system, staring at it blindly, hugging my arms as
though I might fall apart if I let go. A few feet away, Johan
sat on a bench, head bent, being berated by a couple of
uniformed police officers. Their heavy boots and prominent
gun holsters gave me chills. There were no garlands of wildflowers down here, I thought, no crystal clear archipelago
waters. Deep in the bowels of Stockholm, there was angry
graffiti and a stink of piss just like everywhere else.

'Are you okay?' said a soft voice, and I turned to see the
ginger Viking standing behind me. I nodded, not sure if I
could speak. 'This is my sister's phone number,' he added,
pressing a note into my hand. 'If you want to talk to a
woman. She is not trained in anything, she is just a nice
person.'

I nodded again, staring at the note as the numbers swam
before my eyes.

He hesitated a moment, his eyes filled with concern,
then he nodded and left. I glanced over at Johan and saw
that the police had left him. We were alone.

'I guess maybe I should have warned you I was a hooli-
gan,' Johan said quietly, his words echoing in the empty

platform. I tried to raise a ghost of a smile but my face wouldn't quite cooperate.

He sat hunched over, staring at a puddle that might be due to the rain earlier, or going by the smell that pervaded the station, might well have been piss. He looked beaten.

Not literally. There was an angry looking graze on his left cheekbone, the beginnings of a faint bruise on his right temple, but no blood, no real injury. It had been him against three of them in the end, I thought dully. The one who'd made the crack about Johan's team being shit and two of his mates. And Johan was barely injured.

One of them had passed me by a few minutes earlier, leaning heavily on the police officer supporting him, holding a paper towel against his mangled and bloodied nose. Johan had done that, I'd thought, the words echoing meaninglessly around my mind.

I took a couple of steps forward and stood over him, at the far end of the bench. Misery emanated from him, so strongly it was palpable. I was torn, I thought desperately with rising panic. Every fibre of me wanted to go to him, to put my arms around him and make it all better. Every fibre of me wanted to turn and run far, far away.

'It was my girlfriend.'

What?

Was he talking about me? I was his girlfriend. But he wasn't talking about me. A heavy, icy feeling slithered through me, hardening in my veins, beginning to suffocate me. Of course he wasn't talking about me.

'She — who — what you found. On the beach. She was my girlfriend.'

A T-bana train pulled into the station and deposited a handful of commuters. The crowds were long gone now, everyone who was going to the game was already there;

everyone else, it seemed, had hurried home or to the pub to watch with friends. The commuters cleared the platform and Johan and I were alone again.

'She went missing, last September. And you — you found her.'

9

I sat down very suddenly, at the far end of the bench, as far away from Johan as I could. A jubilant cheer sounded somewhere in the distance, echoing around the the empty platform. Somebody had scored a goal. A numb, hollow feeling was spreading through me.

'It was the last weekend in September,' Johan was saying, his voice low and strained, though curiously brisk, as though now he had opened the door to this speech there was no stopping it. 'It was sunny and warm as summer, so we decided to go to Krister's cottage one last time before winter set in. Sanna didn't want to come. There was some party in Stockholm she wanted to go to, one of her friends was launching a new bar in Stureplan. Then at the last moment she changed her mind and came along.

'On the Sunday she wanted to take the early ferry back, about lunchtime, but I was hungover and tired and wanted to enjoy the sun without rushing. We argued a little bit, then she said she would take the kayak out for a while, and I fell asleep in the garden. When I woke and she was not there, I thought she had decided to get the early ferry after all, and

—' He shook his head, a hard, bitter smile playing on his face. 'I was relieved.'

'How would she have got to the ferry?' I asked. I shivered, my mind reeling.

Focus on facts. If I could just gather the facts, sort them into a neat pile, then everything would be okay. 'Krister's boat was presumably still on the island.'

'The kayak,' he replied. 'We use it if someone else needs the boat. It is not so far to the island where the ferry stops, and Sanna knew the way, she had done it before. We tie the kayak beneath the jetty, and the next person brings it back to the island and so on.'

'So it wasn't until you got back to Stockholm that you realised she was missing?'

He nodded. 'It was one day later. That night I went straight home and crashed out. It was not until I finished work the following day that I realised I had not heard from her and started to call her friends.'

Johan worked as a bank teller. I remembered being slightly surprised when he told me that. Not that there's anything wrong with being a bank teller, it just didn't seem to suit him somehow. Then one night he confessed he had wanted to be a nurse but it hadn't worked out. I'd encouraged him to retrain — never too late to follow your dreams and all that, but he'd got a bit shirty about it and we'd dropped the subject.

'They suspected me.' His voice broke. He pressed his fist against his mouth, holding back a sob that threatened to choke him. His knuckles were raw and bloody. I pictured the guy being led away by police, his nose mashed across his face.

'There is a very deep channel that runs between two islands which you must cross to get to the ferry, and the day after we finally called the police, they found the kayak floating upturned there. They sent divers down, of course, but it is a very difficult area to search completely, with many underwater ledges and caves. They concluded she must be trapped somewhere very deep.'

I nodded. I remembered from writing about a drowning in the Thames last year that it's typical for bodies to initially sink to the bottom then gradually rise again and eventually resurface a few weeks later. Unless they were trapped, I thought with a shudder.

'They thought she just tipped out of the kayak at some point?' I asked. 'Wouldn't she have swum to the shore?' I remembered most of the islands being fairly close together. The main thing that had kept me from screaming out loud as Krister drove us to his island was the fact that dry land never seemed particularly far away.

Johan shrugged. 'We had been drinking, and the water was already cold so close to October. It can put you into shock if you fall in fast, you panic, lose your bearings — it happens.'

Tiny tingles of anxiety were breaking out over me. I thought about the macabre sight on the beach that morning. There had been a scrap of bright red fabric clinging to what had once been her shoulder. A sundress, I thought. A pretty sundress she had put on that morning. Maybe with a full skirt that had billowed up around her as she struggled in the icy water, choking on her own terror as she fought for air. I wiggled my fingers a little to try to release the pins and needles, forced myself to take a long, slow breath.

'But they suspected you?'

Johan nodded, his jaw tight. 'I understand,' he said, his voice so strained I barely recognised it. 'I know the statistics for if a woman goes missing or is hurt — of course they must consider her partner. There was a hole in the kayak that we all knew about, it is just old and shit and has been patched many times. When the police found the kayak, the latest patch was gone. It could have just worn away, it probably did, but they questioned me —' he turned to me, his eyes desperate — 'just as a witness, but a piece-of-shit newspaper wrote about it as though I was a suspect and my whole life fell apart.

'Only Liv and Krister and Mia believed me without question. Some of my other friends still do not speak to me, or worse, they smile when they see me but their eyes wonder. I was asked to take a long absence from my job which eventually turned into my job no longer existing. My mother —' he gave a shaky sigh — 'my mother asked me to look her in the eyes and promise her that I was innocent.'

The sob finally overcame him and he bent double, shuddered as it wracked through him. His ragged, choking gasps tore at my heart and I scrabbled across the bench, held him close, stroked his hair as he sobbed.

10

Later that night, the soft lilac glow of the midnight twilight filled the flat as I lay wide awake, listening to Johan's gentle snores, feeling the heat of him next to me.

He didn't have any curtains. Neither did any of his neighbours, as I'd discovered on my second evening there when I'd glanced out the window and been treated to the sight of an elderly woman pottering about her flat across the road, naked as the day she was born. I'd been so mortified I'd burst into a fit of giggles, and Johan's bafflement had made me laugh harder.

'We trust people not to look,' he'd muttered stiffly, and I'd got the hiccups.

Now, I was grateful for the light streaming through the window. I didn't trust my state of mind to darkness. Johan shifted in his sleep, and my heart leapt into my mouth for absolutely no reason. Irritated with myself, I fumbled on the nightstand for my phone and and went over to the sofa, a little away from the sleeping alcove, so as not to disturb Johan. There was a pile of my clothes on the sofa and I felt a stab of guilt as I moved them aside.

Johan's flat was tiny, just one room and kitchen and hall-way. It was smaller than even the pokiest flat I'd known in London, but by virtue of its high ceilings, bright white walls and ingenious use of space, it didn't feel nearly as claustro-phobic as I'd first thought it might be. It was, however, disturbingly pristine.

I'm not overly messy, but I've always liked a bit of cheerful clutter about the place. Knick-knacks, souvenirs and the odd random postcard blu-tacked to my kitchen wall that I've always meant to get around to getting a frame for. Johan's flat, however, looked like a showroom, all clean lines and minimalism, framed black and white prints of city skylines and two or three books artfully posed on a single shelf. At first I thought he must have cleaned up for my arrival, and fully expected to open a cupboard one day to have all manner of smelly boy stuff descend on my head. But nope, what was visible appeared to be all the shit he had. I was in love with a neat freak. It was what it was.

Curling up on the sofa, I started to scroll mindlessly through Facebook. I didn't know what I thought about everything he'd told me that evening. I didn't even know where to begin. My mind felt blank and heavy, as though bits of my brain had turned to lead and I didn't have the energy to force it into thoughts. I thumbed through engage-ment announcements and holiday selfies and the odd abhorrent political rant, clicking to like or love or shed a tear for no particular reason.

None of the Midsummer crew had posted anything in days. A little flutter of something sharp and bitter sprang to life in my stomach as I realised that they had all known. Of course they had. What were the chances a random skeleton had washed up right where their friend disappeared nine months previously? That explained the huddle that didn't include me, the tension zinging in the air I'd chosen to ignore.

Then I noticed that someone had posted something on Johan's wall, just a few minutes earlier. I clicked to translate. Someone named Linda Andersson had written *I am so shit sorry, friend. Sanna was a beautiful person who will live in my heart.* This was followed by a series of heart emojis, presumably in case Johan was unsure as to what she meant by 'heart.' My own heart started to beat a tiny bit faster as I noticed that the word 'Sanna' was bolded. Linda had tagged her in the post. Knowing I was intruding on grief I had no business to, I let my thumb hover over her name for several seconds before I clicked on it and Sanna Johansson's profile loaded.

A nasty part of me almost laughed when I saw her profile picture. A blonde goddess in an itsy bitsy bikini, doing a star jump against a flawlessly blue sky on some idyllic beach somewhere. Of course she bloody was. If I tried to do a star jump in a bikini I'd probably knock myself out with one of my own boobs.

What is the matter with me, I thought in horror. This poor woman was tragically dead at thirty, and here I was, snuggled up on her boyfriend's sofa, resenting her for being hot.

Her wall had turned into a sort of condolence guest book. The comments had been automatically translated, dozens and dozens of variations on *miss you forever, thoughts with your family, cannot believe I will never see your smiling face again.* One comment caught my eye as I passed, and I had to scroll back to find it again.

A Gustav Lindström, who, according to his profile picture, appeared to consist primarily of pecs, had posted *Fy fan Sanna*, followed by a heart emoji. The was no translation available, but the words rang a bell. I remembered Krister shouting it during the Midsummer dinner, when Johan spilled a bottle of beer over him. I'd laughed, and Mia had explained it meant *for fuck's sake*.

I clicked on Gustav Lindström's profile.

It appeared I was correct about him primarily consisting of pecs. His sculpted torso made even Johan look like he had a jiggly dad bod, and the few posts on his wall that were public were of him straining, surprisingly unattractively, to deadlift some spectacular weight or other. His bio identified him as a personal trainer, but if he shared any more personal details than that, they were visible to friends only.

My heart leapt into my mouth as I saw that there was a new post on his wall, posted just seconds ago. Linda Andersson had uploaded a headshot of Sanna smiling into the camera, her eyes sparkling with life and fun. The translation of the caption read *we who loved you Sanna*, and about twenty people were tagged. I opened the list and saw Mia listed, but no Krister or Liv — and no Johan. I grabbed my battered little notebook from my bag and opened to a fresh page.

Why didn't he see the kayak on the way to the ferry? I wrote. I doodled around the edges of the page as I thought. Johan turned over in his sleep, and I froze, but he didn't wake. I thought of the short journey between the ferry stop and Krister's island. The pristine openness of the deep blue water, the untouched islands all around. I couldn't imagine how one would fail to notice a bloody great kayak floating upside down. So had it drifted out of sight then back into the open for the police to find a day or two later?

That struck me as far fetched, and my journalist spidey-senses were tingling. Convoluted murders with dastardly motives and shocking twists are the stuff of police dramas. Real crime tends to be pretty mundane. Straightforward, common-or-garden, someone lashes out in anger, does someone over for money — horrendous and tragic and pretty basic. Kayaks don't turn invisible then conveniently reappear when the police are looking. Statistically, women are horrifically likely to be murdered by their partners, but not by tampering with their kayaks. There was something cold about that. Distant, calculated.

I drew little flowers along the side of the page as Johan snored softly. I suppose everyone looks innocent when they're asleep. Even godfathers of crime don't evilly twirl their moustaches in their sleep, but this was Johan. My Johan.

Now that so much time has passed —
      And whose fault is that?
I'm sorry, but I have to tell you the case is being closed.
How can it be closed? It's not solved.
Well, paused. If any new evidence comes to light —
How will that happen if no one is looking for it? Is this how you solve crimes now, you just sit around and hope that evidence magically appears? How do you sleep at night?
I understand it is difficult, but there must be an avenue of investigation for us to purse.
It wasn't an accident. He was murdered. Don't look at me like that. I know you believe it, you just won't admit it because if you did you would have to get off your fat arse and do something about it.
If you have any information that we can use to —
I've given you information! I told you about her months ago.
Without a name or a description —
Without a name or a description there's nothing you can do. I heard you the first fifty thousand times.

I hated Torsten von Rais from the second I lay eyes on him.

Despite the fact that my mum and I didn't have a pot to piss in, I went to a fancy girls' school across the river in Hammersmith. This was thanks to the deep pockets and guilty conscience of the chinless wonder my mum had pulled at some Chelsea club in the mid eighties. Sn unfortunate night out that resulted in a stonking hangover and me.

I don't doubt that everyone's hearts were in the right place when they decided that I should get the best education he — or more accurately, his family — could afford, but tossing a dash of classism into the viper's nest of a West London all-girls school doesn't exactly make for the warmest and fuzziest of teenage years.

Don't get me wrong, I was fine in the end. I joined a weekend drama club and made some mates who went to the local state school, who didn't snort with laughter and imitate my accent whenever I opened my mouth or refuse to sit with me at lunch. It was just that some days were a bit more character-building than I would have chosen, in an ideal world.

When I was a rookie on the *Evening Standard,* I was sent to doorstep the wife of some guy who'd been done for a financial crime I couldn't make head nor tail of but had resulted in hundreds of people losing their pensions. I banged on the door and lo and behold, it was answered by the queen bee of my school. Emily Something-Double-Barrelled had once filled my backpack with condoms then followed me incessantly with her sniggering friends until eventually, inevitably, they had all fallen out on the top deck of a bus going along the Fulham Palace Road.

'Oh thank goodness it's you,' she'd wailed. 'You won't write anything nasty, will you?'

I did, though. I did write something nasty.

Anyway, all water under the bridge now, but it has left me with a, shall we say, healthy skepticism of posh people. Johan's lawyer Torsten von Rais had hair I can only describe as floufy, and he wore pink trousers, in broad daylight. We were never going to be soulmates.

Torsten, Johan and I were having coffee in an area that I could see a mile off was the Chelsea of Stockholm, only with more bikes and tall people. I'd thought that Södermalm was all pristine and fancy, but it was practically a concrete jungle compared to the grand, gleaming white buildings and wide boulevards of Östermalm, the stomping ground of Torsten von Rais.

I stirred my coffee and licked the chocolate off the back of the spoon, enjoying Torsten's brief disapproving glance, as he opened his soft leather, embossed notebook, and took out a fountain pen.

'The tests the coroner was able to do were somewhat limited, given the advanced state of decomposition of the body,' he said, in a clipped accent. I felt Johan flinch, and reached over to squeeze his hand. 'But there is a jelly in the back of the eye socket which tends to be the last to decay, and they were able to extract DNA for the identification. They also detected traces of drugs —'

'Drugs?' Johan's head snapped up. 'Absolutely not.'

Torsten shrugged, his eyes impassive. 'That is what the tests indicate.'

'No.' Johan shook his head firmly. 'Sanna's best friend died of an overdose five or six years ago. She was vehemently anti-drugs. It is just not possible.'

'Be that as it may, the tests are conclusive.'

'It's not true,' Johan said. 'What if it's not Sanna? Could the — it, could it be someone else who drowned last summer also?'

'The identification is certain. The police have checked both dental records and DNA.'

'She wouldn't,' Johan insisted, shaking his head. 'We were drinking, but absolutely nothing else.'

'What drugs did they find in her system?' I asked.

'I would have to check the exact name of the substance, but I believe it is some sort of sedative, often used in the treatment of anxiety.'

'Something like diazepam?' I asked.

'Yes, I think so,' Torsten nodded.

'Could she have had a prescription?' I asked Johan.

'Sanna wasn't afraid of anything,' he said firmly, and something icy twisted in my stomach.

'What if she didn't take them voluntarily?' I said. 'If we're talking foul play, she could have been drugged. It's not uncommon for killers to sedate their victims.'

'What killer?' Johan demanded and I shrugged.

'I don't know, I'm just —'

'That is not something one can establish from the jelly in the back of the eye,' Torsten said, with the tiniest tug of his lips that could have been a smile or a grimace. 'And there is very little further physical evidence in the case at all. The police are not certain whether the patch on the kayak fell off or was removed, and as I understand it, all of your friends' statements have been consistent and have not revealed anything the police consider an avenue of investigation.'

They were all there? I hadn't realised that. Johan must have said, I thought, though I could have sworn I'd got the impression it was just the two of them.

'The important thing is, I think it is unlikely at this point that the police will charge you with any crime,' Torsten said, gathering up papers and putting them back in his soft leather briefcase. 'There is simply not enough evidence.'

'Because he is innocent,' I said.

Torsten didn't respond, but I felt condescension emanate from him in waves.

'What about his job, in that case?' I added.

'What about his job?'

'Ellie, it doesn't matter,' Johan muttered.

'It does,' I said. 'He lost his job because of this suspicion that's been hanging over him. The police need to make some sort of statement, properly exonerate him —'

'I don't really think that is the sort of thing the police —'

'And I think we should sue.'

'I beg your pardon?'

'For wrongful termination. They can't go around firing people because some idiot journalist got the wrong end of the stick. I should know, I'm an idiot journalist.'

'This is your job at *Södersjukhuset*?' Torsten asked Johan, consulting his notes with a frown. Johan nodded uncomfortably.

'It's not —' Johan began, before muttering something in Swedish.

Torsten nodded, and replied in Swedish.

'Do you mind?' I snapped. 'I'm sitting right here.'

'My apologies,' said Torsten, his pale hazel eyes cool. 'Johan was explaining to me that his employment was terminated when he made a mistake in reporting some results from a clinical trial of a new drug. Understandable in grief perhaps, but you must appreciate that a hospital cannot tolerate such mistakes.'

I turned to Johan with a frown, a bolt of nerves shooting down my spine. *I always wanted to be a nurse, but it didn't work out.* Johan stared at the table, refusing to meet my eye.

A bunch of pastel colour-shirted guys at the next table gave a rowdy cheer, raising their glasses with shouts of *skål*. On the centre of their table was a huge platter of mussels. The salty smell made me feel sick.

'I do not think it is likely we will have a good outcome if we sue the Swedish medical system,' Torsten said dryly, putting the lid back on his fountain pen with an irritating click. 'But as for the police matter, I believe it is concluded, until or unless new evidence comes to light. Just perhaps do not annoy them by getting into fights on the T-bana in the meantime,' he added with a glance at Johan.

'Oh for heaven's sake, a drunken punch up between football fans is hardly the same as murdering your girlfriend,' I snapped, and Torsten gave me a cold look.

'All violence is on a spectrum,' he said quietly, and left.

13

We walked home in silence. Somewhere along the cobblestoned quay in the Old Town, I realised I was totally overreacting. *I wanted to be a nurse, but it didn't work out.* He had told me the truth. It wasn't his fault I had misunderstood.

I'd been about to slip my hand into his then, but his hands were deep in his pockets, his eyes troubled and faraway as he gazed out over the water. He was lost in thoughts that didn't involve me. That was fine. It was a lot for him to take in.

I was now sitting cross legged on the couch, while Johan dusted invisible dust from his shelf of three books. I swear that shelf got more polishing action than my entire flat in London. I pulled out my notebook and flicked to a new page. 'How did you first meet Sanna?'

'Does it matter?'

'To start building a full picture of what happened, yes.'

'We met through Mia.'

That explained why she had been tagged in the list of people who loved Sanna the other night on Facebook.

'How did they know each other?'

Johan shrugged, putting his pile of books back in precisely the same order. 'Through work. Mia works with events, organising parties and launches for new products and things. Sanna was a DJ.'

I'd already gathered as much from her social media, but I scribbled it down anyway.

'Did Mia set you up?'

'No, not really. She just got me and Krister and Liv on the guest list for the opening night of a new bar she was involved with. It was summer and seemed like fun so we went along. Sanna was DJing, and when she took a break we started talking at the bar.'

'How long ago was that?'

'One year ago, I suppose.'

'Just last summer?'

They'd only been together a few months.

'Yes. A couple of weeks before Midsummer.'

'And what was the relationship like?' I asked.

He was polishing around the TV, and he paused, glanced up at me.

'Come on Johan, I don't mean how many times a week or in what position. I mean like, did you fight like cat and dog the whole time? Was it love's young dream? Just a general idea.'

I met his eye with a deliberately even gaze, my pen poised over the notebook.

He shrugged. 'I don't know, it was okay. Not so serious, just, fun, I guess.'

'No major issues, stuff you fought about time and time again?'

'Nothing that would make me want to kill her,' he said

abruptly. He went into the kitchen, and I could hear him banging about, probably polishing apples or something.

'But you fought the weekend she disappeared?' I called after him. 'You said that the other night.'

'Yes. So what?'

'So you did fight sometimes.'

'Ellie, what is the point of all of this?' he sighed. He stood in the open doorway between the living room and the hall, almost silhouetted by the light from the kitchen window behind him.

I didn't say anything.

'I told you, she didn't want to come that weekend. She wanted to stay with her friends in the city. I wish she had.'

'What changed her mind?'

'I don't know.'

'She just randomly told you she was coming after all? You didn't talk her into it?'

'I told you, I don't know Ellie. She said no, then she texted me the night before to ask what time we were getting the ferry, so I guessed she was coming. She did that a lot, changing plans according to what mood she was in that day.'

'Okay.' I tapped my pen against the notebook. 'On the day you went — the Saturday, I assume?' He nodded. 'Was it just you and her on the ferry?'

'And Liv also. Mia and Krister went the night before.'

I bet Liv loved that, I thought. Thinking she'd get Johan to herself for the whole journey, then lo and behold the girl-friend shows up.

'How did Sanna seem?'

'Hungover. She had been working the night before, then she partied after. She slept most of the way.'

'You said you argued a lot during the weekend. Was it over something specific?'

'Not really. Just — I don't know, bickering. Like I said, she was hungover and kind of grouchy and I felt like she was ruining things for Mia and Krister.'

'Ruining what?'

'They just got engaged earlier that week and we were celebrating them, but it did not feel like much of a celebration. Mia likes to fix things for everybody, so she spent most of the weekend trying to explain Sanna to me and me to Sanna.'

'What about any tension between Sanna and any of the others?'

'Are you accusing one of my friends of murdering her?' His tone was dry, but there was an edge to it.

'Of course not,' I said shortly. 'I'm just trying to build a picture of the weekend. She might have mentioned a worry to one of them, or —.'

'No, there was no tension between her and anyone else.'

'Would you normally have been able to see the kayak tied to the jetty?'

'What?'

'You said that you all use this kayak to get back and forth between the ferry stop and Krister's island. If Sanna had taken it over to get the early ferry like you thought, would you normally have seen it tied up there?'

'I don't know. It depends. It could have been under the jetty. I wasn't really looking for it.'

'Even though you thought she had left it there?'

'For fuck's sake Ellie, what is the point of this?'

Johan turned to the kitchen door and slammed it with a ferocity that reverberated through the flat. I flinched, my heart hammering, as the almighty bang rang in my ears.

Johan stood in the hallway, his shoulders hunched in defeat, staring at the door.

'I'm just trying to — '

'Just stop,' he said quietly, his voice laced with pleading. 'Leave it alone.'

'You told me you didn't want people to look at you and wonder any more,' I said. I stared at my notebook, the words swimming before my eyes.

'I'm going to make dinner,' he blurted. 'Is pasta okay?'

'I'm going out, actually.'

I shut my notebook and shoved it in my bag, rooted around for my sandals. 'Some of the crowd from that newcomers coffee group I told you about are having drinks.'

I'm sure I imagined the flicker of relief in his eyes. He smiled, though his eyes were still wretched.

'So I will start to make dinner for me.' He came over to me as I put my trainers on, kissed the top of my head, held my face close to him for a moment.

'I know you are trying to help,' he said. 'Thank you. I'm sorry I am so —'

'Enjoy the peace,' I said as I closed the door behind me.

14

Maybe by the time I get home you'll be ready to face this like an adult.

The parting shot I should have gone with rattled around my head for almost the entire length of Södermalm. That was the problem. Johan wanted to close his eyes and stick his fingers in his ears and make it all go away, I could see that clearly now. That was why he had kept it all from me, why he had broken off contact with anyone who questioned him. He wanted to pretend none of it was real.

I'd seen it before. Grieving mothers putting on a spectacular spread of home baking to entertain parasitic journalists, families of the accused talking brightly about the holiday they would take together once this nasty business was all over. The human capacity for denial is powerful, but it's like taking painkillers for an infected wound. You might not be able to feel the pain, but it's going septic all the same.

I crossed the footbridge onto the little island of Långholmen where Sanna's memorial was being held. The narrow canal that separate the smaller island from Södermalm was lined with speedboats, some flashy and new, others rickety and wooden. Johan's family owned one of them, I remembered. He'd told me that no one had used it in years, but that his mother dutifully fixed it up each spring just in case. He had promised he would take me out in it soon, to which I'd smiled and nodded and decided that 'soon' would be 'never.'

With one last look at the boats, I shuddered and pulled out my phone to check the directions. Good old Linda Andersson had tagged Mia and Gustav Lindström in the Facebook event that morning. Johan wasn't on the guest list for the event, but he must have seen it. All morning I'd been half on tenterhooks, wondering if he would announce he was going. Or worse, claim to be meeting Krister for a drink or something, and instead come here.

Which was in fact what I had done.

But for good reason, I reminded myself as I approached the crowd gathered in what looked like a little picnic clearing. Through the trees I could just spot the crooked roofs and steeples of the Old Town across the huge expanse of calm, inky water, shrouded in shadow under the pinks and purples of the sunset. I spotted a red pleasure balloon floating high overhead, cruelly incongruous against the muted atmosphere of the gathering. Somewhere just out of sight some evening swimmers were screaming and splashing.

The crowd was predictably glamorous. It would be difficult to identify a trendy Stockholmer in mourning, I thought, they seemed to dress head to toe in black regardless of their emotional state. In fact, I realised as I accepted what seemed to be an order of service from a quietly sobbing girl, I was the only one in the entire crowd not wearing some variation of a black leather jacket. I quickly covered my face with the card so as to hide my ghost of a smile.

It would be extremely handy if there was some kind of app that could translate live conversation. Eavesdropping proves something of a challenge when you don't understand a bloody word of what's being said, but even so, as I moved through the crowd, pretending to be looking for friends to join, I was picking up a vibe. There were one or two women in tears, a couple of clumps of people standing solemnly with their arms around one another, but I wasn't picking up on deep or untamed sorrow.

It could be that after nine months the initial horror had numbed, but in my experience, even after someone has been missing a long time, the discovery of the body tears apart any semblance of closure, exposes the rawness of grief. I'd once covered the memorial of a minor associate of the Krays' who had gone missing sometime in the late sixties. His body had finally been found when they bull-dozed a warehouse in Bethnal Green and uncovered the remains of several henchmen in the concrete floor. Nearly half a century later, his widow, brothers and kids who hadn't seen him since they were toddlers, were howling as though he'd dropped dead in front of them they day before.

If I had to put money on it, I'd say that not many people here knew Sanna particularly well, much less truly gave a monkey's about her. There was something performative about the mournful expressions, the silver candles that were being passed out and held aloft like at a stadium rock gig. It was like a terribly stylish performance art funeral, the sort of thing pretentious idiots would queue round the block in Shoreditch or Brooklyn to witness. Most of the tears I could see were what an old editor of mine used to call reality TV tears, glistening eyes hinting at emotion, but nowhere near enough to run the risk of ruining impeccable eye makeup.

That didn't reflect badly on Sanna, necessarily. I'd had my own club days once upon a time, in the heady years of my early twenties when I would roll in from Ministry at dawn and be chugging Red Bull at the news desk of wherever I had blagged a week's freelancing at an hour later. For about three years I existed on toast, caffeine and enough Columbian marching powder to fell a horse, and I wondered why I didn't manage to form a functional relationship with an adult human male in all that time.

Not that I was remotely fussed about that then. I was having much too much fun waking up next to a succession of skinny boys with pretentious indie boy haircuts and politely enquiring as to why they were wearing my pants. If I'm honest though, I didn't have a single real friend during that period either, and it didn't take Freud to figure out that I stuffed my loneliness up my nose.

That's just the nature of that scene though. It's all shadowy strangers, ships that pass in the ladies', the love of the night based on whomever still had the digital dexterity to unbutton my jeans come kicking-out time. It was what it was. Aren't everyone's twenties a bit messy? This lot seemed a bit too shiny-haired to be sinking to the cheerful depths I did, but I sensed a detachment that was chillingly familiar.

I'd managed to find Gustav Lindström's Instagram earlier that afternoon, and though it gave no hint of his life beyond the fact that he liked to lift heavy shit and was inordinately fond of protein shakes, there had been a couple of decent headshots. I was scanning the crowd for him, wondering if I would detect true grief etched on his face, or if he'd be like the guy I was passing now, his eyes closed, face contorted in a way I assumed was intended to convey

deep emotion but actually made him look severely consti-
pated. Maybe it was too painful for Gustav to come at all, I
thought, and a coldness seeped through me as I wondered if
that was why Johan wasn't here.

'Hey, Ellie,' called a voice, and I turned to see Mia
heading for me. My heart sank. 'I didn't know you were
coming,' she said, enveloping me in a hug. 'Is Johan here?'

'No, he — it was just — because I found her —' I impro-
vised wildly. 'I felt I should be here. I hope I'm not
intruding.'

'You have such a kind heart,' she said, smiling though
her tears. She stroked my hair with an odd, faraway look in
her eyes, and I stood there awkwardly, not wanting to inter-
rupt her grief. 'Sanna was so full of life,' she said. 'So fun. I
just can't quite —'

She gave a shaky breath, and I squeezed her hand,
feeling like the most callous person ever to walk the
planet.

'You would have loved her,' she added, then thankfully
turned away before she could see my expression. Given that
she was going out with my boyfriend — or I was going out
with hers — I felt that things between us would have been
socially awkward to say the least. It felt churlish to point
that out given the circumstances, so I stayed quiet.

A few moments later, the crowd quietened and a little
guy with long, straight blond hair that made him look a bit
like a miniature version of Legolas, stepped onto a stone
mound. He looked vaguely familiar, and I wondered if I had
seen him in one of Sanna's Facebook photos. He began to
speak, his voice low, but steady and confident. He was used
to public speaking. The crowd was rapt, a couple of muted
chuckles here and there.

'That is Olaf,' Mia whispered. 'Sanna's brother.'

That was why he looked familiar, I realised. The family resemblance was strong.

'He is talking about how crazy Sanna could be,' Mia continued softly. 'She persuaded him to climb onto the roof of their family's house when they were children. He fell and broke his leg and she felt so guilty she also used crutches for the entire summer.'

Olaf's speech was followed by a few people Mia informed me were colleagues, an old school friend, her yoga teacher. Mia whispered running translations of their Sanna anecdotes, all painting a picture of a warm, funny, kind hearted, generally perfect person. Of course, to be fair, it was her funeral. How likely would it be that speakers would take the opportunity to air their grievances?

The last speech over, the crowd began to disperse and Mia was greeted by a couple dressed alike in black jeans and the requisite black leather jackets. I took the opportunity to have a final scan for Gustav Lindström, and suddenly found myself face to face with Olaf.

'I'm so sorry for your loss,' I muttered, touching his arm. He withdrew it as though I were filthy.

'Is it true you are Johan's girlfriend?' he spat.

'Yes, I —' I stammered. I glanced around for Mia but she had disappeared into the shadows.

'What are you doing here? Are you spying for him?'

'No, of course not, absolutely not,' I said in horror. 'I just — I'm so sorry, I —'

'Get out of here. Go home and fuck your murderer.'

I turned and ran.

15

He was the love of my life. That's such a cliché, I know, but as many of you know, he was the boy next door and I adored him long before I knew that that meant. He didn't adore me, of course, not back then. He thought that girls were weird and annoying and he ignored me for years. It broke my heart of course, but deep down I wasn't worried. Deep down, I knew that our time would come. And it did.

After university I went travelling, hoping, perhaps, to try to forget him, maybe even meet someone new. But everything — sunsets in Nepal, the mountains of Bali, the Great Barrier Reef — all made me think of him, made me wish he was there to share it with me.

Then I got home and there he was. Finally. He had missed me. Had finally seen what I had known since we were six years old. We had eight, perfect, precious years together.

Often, he would talk about the years we had missed out on, how he wished he had seen sooner, that we could have shared more —

That is why I know that he would never leave me.

I know this isn't what today is for — I know I promised I

wouldn't — but I have to. Those of you who are here today knew him the best, loved him the most — you must know what I do, that he wouldn't leave any of us. The police won't listen any more but I can't —

Please — I'm not finished, I have more to say — just one more moment, I promise I won't —

In fact, no. No. Why am I lying? I can't promise. I won't promise.

I promise the opposite. I promise never to give up. To fight for him until my dying day. Until the truth comes out. I have nothing left. He is gone. I have nothing to lose.

16

I walked blindly for goodness knows how long, propelled through quiet streets by horror and shock and guilt. The shadows were long but the sky was still a blinding white, and as I felt tears building I cursed the bloody Swedish summer. If I were at home at least I'd have the privacy of darkness to have a good old cry.

I blundered my way to the park where Johan and I had sat with ice creams in that first week, when he told me about his grandparents working at the button factory. I walked along the waterfront and into the trees, until I found a tiny patch of sand where I sat down and stared out blindly at the glass-like lake. It was a perfectly still night, the full moon in the pale blue sky reflecting on the shimmering water. On the opposite shore was a row of modern blocks of flats, stark white boxes surrounded by deep green pine trees.

I didn't want to cry. This wasn't my thing to cry about. I didn't even know the woman. I watched a couple of ducks land on the water, silhouetted by the fading light, causing ripples to cascade all the way to my tiny beach for one, and realised that wasn't entirely true.

Sanna hadn't wanted to come to Krister's that weekend. She'd wanted to leave as early as possible. That sounded familiar. Could it have been because she had already spent plenty of weekends being ignored by Liv and patronised by Krister? Johan had said she spent the whole time in a bad mood. Hadn't I found her precisely because I'd retreated from them in a bad mood? Unlike me Sanna would have been able to understand their conversation, but I had a sneaking suspicion that not even fluent Swedish would have made twenty years' worth of in-jokes accessible to an outsider.

I'd been desperate to leave. If I hadn't been so terrified of boats, would the kayak have crossed my mind? I could see Sanna, in my mind's eye, in her red sundress, blinking back tears as she yanked the kayak into the water and climbed aboard. Telling herself Johan didn't mean to be distant in the company of his friends, that he didn't understand what it felt like to be the odd one out. Promising herself she would talk to him properly when they got back to Stockholm, make him understand that she wanted to be with him, not his friends. Maybe it was finally bursting into tears that made the kayak capsize, plunging her forever into the ice-cold depths.

'Ellie! Shit, I am so glad I found you.' Mia sat down next to me and put her arm around my shoulders. 'Are you okay? I wasn't sure if I should call Johan, I was so worried.'

'I'm fine,' I muttered. 'I just needed to get away. It was my fault. I should never have intruded.'

'I heard about what Olaf said to you. I should not have left you alone, I never thought that he would even recognise you. I am so sorry. Of course he is crazy with grief. You cannot take anything he says seriously.'

I nodded. 'I understand,' I said. My voice echoed curiously dull in my own ears. 'I can't begin to imagine what he is going through.'

'It is so terrible. Olaf was the only one who never gave up hope. Of course we all knew months ago what must have happened, but he kept insisting that she was either somewhere in the archipelago with a head injury and no memory, or that she had come back to Stockholm and got on a plane for a new life.'

Got on a plane for a new life? No one does that in real life, surely.

'Why would he think that?' I asked.

Mia shrugged. 'I don't know if he actually believed it as much as just needed to pretend,' she said. 'They did not always have such a good relationship, I think he is dealing with a lot of guilt as well as grief. The poor guy is just turned inside out.'

'I suppose it's easier to blame Johan than deal with what he is feeling,' I said.

'Absolutely. I am sure he does not believe it really, no one who truly knows Johan believes. You know that, don't you? It was just stupid, cruel gossip.'

I nodded. The sky had turned a deep pink. A motorboat chugged slowly across the shimmering water into a nearby jetty. 'Does Olaf know Johan well, then?'

'Not really, they met a few times when Sanna and Johan were together. But he knows he did not kill her.'

'Why?' I asked. 'If he doesn't know Johan well?'

'Because anyone who thinks Johan killed anybody is stupid,' said Mia firmly.

I nodded. A chilly breeze danced through the trees, and I shivered. Somewhere nearby, some ducks squawked contentedly.

'Were he and Sanna happy together?' I asked.

Mia thought a moment before answering. 'Maybe, I'm not sure. They were new. It's always wonderful and terrifying when it is new, isn't it?'

I smiled tightly, hugging my knees for warmth. 'I suppose so.'

'He was not happy like he is with you.'

'I wonder,' I said softly.

'Oh there is no question. I have known Johan since many, many years and I have never seen him as he is with you. He comes alive when he looks at you. You are the love of his life.'

My smile froze. I knew she was being kind, but — but it was ridiculous. We had known one another for less than seven months, five and a bit of which consisted of snatched weekends in London and a lot of Skype sex. We couldn't be the loves of one another's lives yet. We hadn't even weathered our first storm.

'We have been so worried about him, Krister and I, and Liv too. He has been a shadow of himself for so many months, and we are so grateful to you for bringing our friend back to us.'

'Any time,' I said with a forced grin.

'You promise you will not worry about what Olaf said? I am sure he already feels terrible.'

'I sincerely hope I am the last thing on his mind,' I said firmly. 'I'd better get home,' I added, getting to my feet and brushing the sand off my skirt. 'Johan will be wondering where I am.'

17

There are few places more depressing than a club during the day. At the height of my clubbing days, I worked here and there for promoters I'd got friendly with. I ran the guest list on the door at a few clubs, taking pleasure in letting in hen dos from Essex chancing their luck, and telling reality TV stars and obnoxious breakfast DJs to fuck off. I'd only get away with it a few times before the promoters got wind that I was infecting their glitzy fantasies with actual human people and sack me, but it was so worth it.

I even took up the odd spot of podium dancing when I was seriously skint. I only worked a handful of shifts as a podium dancer, but it left me with the permanent affliction of dancing bitch face. Seriously, ten years later and the minute I hit a dance floor my face just goes ice cold and there's nothing I can do about it. My friends have had to explain to startled tourists that I'm not angry with them, and once I caused a whole wedding party of small children to start crying in fear.

Sometimes in those days, I'd have to pop by the club

during the day to check the rota or pick up cash-in-hand wages, and trust me, you do not want to see the grotty tat behind the wizard's curtain. In the dark, when the the music is pounding and drinks are flowing, literal smoke and mirrors create magic. In the harsh light of day, it's like seeing your Hollywood idol up close. Nobody wants to see the lipstick bleeding into crevices around their mouth or the tit tape holding their face up by the ears.

The Stureplan club where I waited for Linda Andersson the following day was no exception. I sat on a silver barstool by a black formica bar that probably shimmered beguilingly after a few shots. The walls were draped in black satin and the velvet couches took on a cheap sheen under the glare of the overhead lights.

'*Hej* Ellie, so nice to meet you!'

In her social media profile picture, Linda Andersson stared moodily at the camera like a mid-nineties heroin chic model, her slash of dark lipstick looking almost black in the grainy shot. In person, she grinned brightly as she held out her hand to me. Her hair was pulled into a messy ponytail back from a makeup-free face, and she wore jeans — probably designer, but still — and a Ramones T shirt.

'Would you like a coffee?'

I nodded and she went behind the bar to fire up the gleaming coffee machine. 'I am so happy you got in touch. I can't believe you worked at almost every club in London that I loved, I am so jealous. My friends and I would save up for the cheapest flight over as often as we could. We wouldn't even get a hotel because we would just dance all night then sit in a café in Soho drinking coffee until we had to go to the airport. It was wonderful, except when the hangover began on the coach about halfway to Luton. Then I would want to die.'

'Everyone feels that ways about coaches to Luton, even when stone cold sober,' I smiled as she handed me a coffee.

'So what sort of thing were you thinking about doing here? I don't exactly have a job to offer you, but perhaps we could put something together. Do you have an idea?'

In my email to her that morning, I'd hinted vaguely about wanting to start a London-style club night — whatever that meant — in Stockholm. I stalled for time by taking a sip of my coffee, then distracted her with some chat about DJs and promoters I was sure she would have heard of. She turned out to be promisingly amenable to gossip.

We exchanged stories of bar staff overcharging drunk customers then pocketing the difference, DJs who charge a fortune then rock up and play a playlist off their phone, and celebrities who demand an extra VIP area inside the VIP area, in case anyone less famous than them tries to talk to them. Linda told me about the extremely famous Swedish actor who was so jet lagged when he showed up at her club that he fell asleep on a sofa next to the dance floor, dead to the world, spread eagled, snoring and drooling in front of a hundred fascinated people. She'd had to spend the whole night running around confiscating people's phones so that pictures weren't leaked.

'I was just reading something about a Stockholm DJ this week,' I said finally, when I'd finished telling her about the famously happily married DJ who used to demand groupies blew him under the decks while he was playing. 'She drowned or something, I think. Sounded awful. You didn't know her, did you?'

'Sanna,' Linda said, with a sad smile that actually reached her eyes. 'Yes, she was a very good friend. I don't know if you knew, but she was missing for many months,.

We didn't really hold out any hope of her being okay any more, but it was still a shock.'

'Such a tragedy,' I murmured. 'I've never thought of kayaking as an extreme sport, but I suppose you never know the minute.'

'It was not an accident,' said Linda, her voice hard suddenly.

'Oh shit, I'm sorry — I thought I read —'

'No, I'm sorry. It's not your fault he got away with it.'

'Excuse me?'

'Her boyfriend killed her. Staged it to look like an accident. He did it well enough that there is no evidence for the police to charge him with, but that does not make him innocent.'

'How could you be sure, then?' I made a production out of finishing my coffee, praying she couldn't hear my heart thudding in my chest.

'He drugged her. Gave her some type of sedative that made her pass out and fall into the water. He was a nurse. He had access to those sorts of drugs, would know exactly how to use them.'

'That's hardly proof he —'

'I never met the guy, but I have friends who knew them together and he was a fucking weirdo. Jealous, insecure. She was way out of his league and he knew it. She had met someone new, and was going to dump him that weekend. She told me the Friday night before she left. He must have snapped, made sure she could never leave him.'

'You can't possibly —'

'He might have got away with it for now, but they will get him sooner or later. Or,' she shrugged, her eyes cold and hard, 'he will do it again.'

Ten minutes later, I didn't realise how badly my hands

were shaking until I fumbled for my purse on the bus and dropped it twice. The driver was glaring daggers at me by the time I finally managed to tap my Travelcard on the machine, and he pulled out so fast I nearly went flying.

Obviously, Linda Andersson had no idea what she was talking about. The bus swung around Kungsträdgården and the sparkling waters of Stockholm's harbour came in to view. She said herself she hadn't even met Johan. She didn't know him from Adam, and whoever else claimed they 'knew them together' were clearly talking out of their arse. Johan was a lot of things — grumpy and uncommunicative sprang to mind — but insecure and jealous?

No.

Capable of murdering a woman rather than have her chuck him after a summer fling? Absolutely not.

Definitely not.

The day after we met, I was already basically head over heels in love with him, but I was trying to do the cool girl thing, so at some point in the afternoon I left him dozing in the beach hut and wandered back out to the third day of the Full Moon Party. I ran into some people I knew from the hostel I'd been staying at the week before, one thing led to another, and the next thing I knew, was not in a state to operate heavy machinery. After a while I lost track of my friends, and was dancing by myself at the edge of the crowd when I heard an Australian guy slur, 'Meredith?'

Which I ignored, on account of not being Meredith.

'So this is where you escaped to.'

The voice was suddenly a lot closer. Squinting in the darkness, I could just make out a tallish guy wearing not much other than one of those luminous necklaces, thick dirty blond hair in dreds. He was staring at me, wobbling a bit — he definitely shouldn't be operating heavy machinery either — and he appeared to be pissed off with me. It's hardly unheard of for someone I don't know to be pissed off with me, so I asked him what the problem was.

He appeared to be under the impression that my name was Meredith, that I was from California, and that he had bought me four drinks that evening which he appeared to believe that entitled him to my company. For some reason, I chose to deal with this by putting on a mad Valley Girl accent in an attempt to prove I was not, in fact, remotely American. This succeeded in both confusing him and irritating him further. He got shirty and I lost patience, pointing out that four drinks entitled him to precisely nothing, regardless of whether or not I was Meredith. Which, also, I still wasn't.

He started to shout and at one point grabbed my arm and tried to yank me closer, then Johan flew out of the darkness and let's just say told the Aussie to leave me alone, on no uncertain terms. This was met with much the reaction you would expect, and the two of them ended up knocking over a little stall selling energising juices like the pair of brawling idiots they were. I helped the Thai sisters who ran the stall to clean up, and bought all the juices Johan and the other halfwit had spilled. By the time I was finished, the Aussie guy's mates had dragged him off and Johan was sitting on the sand looking sheepish.

As well he should.

So, I've seen him be a hot headed fuckwit on more than one occasion. There was no denying the guy had a temper, and a moronic one at that. I've never said he was perfect, but the guy Linda described — that just wasn't Johan.

Probably someone spotted him and Sanna having a drunken argument once upon a time, or maybe Sanna had a bit of a moan about him being a pain in the arse and they'd got the wrong end of the stick. One whisper turned into another, and suddenly it was established fact Johan was a nasty piece of work. I've seen it happen so many times. Hell, I've probably contributed to it my fair share of times.

None of it meant anything. None of them knew Johan like I did.

The bus swung around Slussen and started to climb the hill towards Johan's flat. As Stockholm's harbour came into view, bathed in the dusky pink of sunset, a thought struck me and suddenly my breath caught in my throat.

What if it wasn't idle gossip that took a dangerous turn when Sanna drowned? What if it suited someone very well for people to believe that Sanna's boyfriend was jealous and prone to violence?

Who was Sanna was about to dump Johan for?

Gustav Lindström and all his pecs popped into my mind.

For fuck's sake, Sanna.

18

The smell hit me as I was kicking off my shoes. Brick Lane. Spices. Don't ask me to be more specific than that, my idea of cooking is grating cheese over baked beans, but whatever it was, it was heavenly.

Johan was in the kitchen, wearing an actual apron over his jeans and baby blue T shirt. He was leaning over a huge, steaming pot on the stove, frowning as he measured out a precise teaspoon of a fiery red spice.

'You said you missed curry,' he said as I came up behind him and slipped my arms around his waist. I leaned my head between his shoulder blades, felt the muscles of his back ripple beneath my cheek as he stirred the burbling mixture. He put the lid on the pot then turned around in my arms and kissed the top of my head. We stood there a moment, just hugging, and I felt relief flood through me. This was my Johan.

His T shirt was soft and smelled clean and fresh, of washing powder scented with a summer's day. He wrapped one arm around my waist, holding me close, and his other hand toyed with my hair, winding a tendril round and round his finger in the way he knew sent shivers down my spine. I rubbed his back and his every muscle felt so achingly familiar it brought a lump to my throat.

'How was your day?' he asked into my hair, and I flinched, guilt unfurling in my stomach. I pulled away and got wine glasses down from the shelf, poured the red that was sitting on the counter behind him. 'Do you think you got the job?'

Right. Yes. I'd told him I had an interview.

'Hard to tell,' I said with what I hoped looked like a hopeful smile as I handed him his wine glass. 'Fingers crossed.'

'I was surprised anyone was interviewing in summer,' he said. I looked up sharply, but there was no suspicion in his eyes. 'Most offices are now almost closed until summer.'

'Yeah, they — they mentioned that. It's something to do with it being freelance, it's a bit more irregular,' I muttered, as though this made a blind bit of sense.

'Well, do not worry if it is not right for you,' he said. 'There is no hurry.'

'My savings aren't going to last forever. There's the small matter of earning money to pay for shit.'

'I pay for this apartment whether you are here or not. You don't even eat much,' he grinned.

That wasn't strictly true. It was just that, left to my own devices, I could quite cheerfully exist on cereal and the odd takeaway, whereas Johan was a stickler for cooking and eating actual meals like some kind of grown up.

'I'm going to pay my way, Johan,' I said firmly, 'I've always paid my way.'

'Of course.' He leaned over to plant a soft kiss on my lips

which I didn't deserve. 'I am only saying you don't need to rush it. Wait for the right job. It is better I pay for the apartment for two or three months more and you find work that makes you happy.' He shrugged. 'If that's what you want. It's up to you.'

'Well, we'll see,' I said, an uncomfortable feeling prickling over me, because here I was arguing with him and I hadn't applied for a single job yet.

'It's not as though you have just been sitting around relaxing,' he added, turning around to stir the pot again. I hopped up to sit on the kitchen counter next to the stove, watched him frowning in concentration as he tasted the mixture then rummaged amongst his spice jars for the one he wanted. 'Mia told me you went to the memorial.'

Mia. Shit. I'd meant to ask her not to say anything to Johan, and I'd clean forgotten.

'Johan —' I began, with zero idea of what to say next.

'It means so much, that you are trying to help me. I thought —' his voice wavered a tiny bit then, and he stared into the curry, as though stirring took an inordinate amount of focus. 'I have been waiting for you to say that you were leaving. Going back to London. I would understand. I would not blame you.'

'Bugger right off.'

He looked up with a surprised grin. 'What?'

'Get lost, if you think you're getting rid of me that easily. Especially not now you've told me it's a cushty gig as a lady of leisure.'

He chuckled and I leaned over and kissed his shoulder.

'But really, I don't know if even 'thank you' is enough to say —'

'Tell you what, you can thank me with a gorgeous curry any time you like.'

He smiled, but I could see in his eyes there was something more, and my stomach twisted with anticipation. Had he found out I'd spoken to Linda, too? Did he know what that shower of Östermalm arseholes were saying about him?

'I am going to get therapy,' he said, levelling off a teaspoon of what looked like hot chocolate powder. 'I have known for many years that I need to, but I — I think I hoped maybe I would mellow in my old age.' He gave a slightly bitter smile. 'I have not.'

'Because of the T-bana fight?'

He nodded, frowned at the curry.

'I think that would be a really good idea,' I said softly, reaching over to stroke his cheek with my thumb. He turned and kissed the palm of my hand. 'And if you want to — I mean, you don't have to, but if you want to talk to me too, I'm here.'

He nodded, stirred the curry some more.

'It is not a very interesting story,' he said finally. 'Quite cliché. My father liked to shout with his fists when he was drunk.' Johan shrugged, but there was a tension I could see in his jaw that tore at my heart. 'It would get bad, my mother would throw him out, then he would come back and it would be okay until the next time. He didn't hit us, usually. He would smash up furniture, would be brought home by police after bar fights.' Johan gave a bitter smile. 'Does that sound familiar?'

I didn't know what to say, so I just took his hand, held it tight.

'What happened to him?' I asked softly.

'He was hit by a car in the freeway that runs through a tunnel under the island. A hit and run. How he got down there, who knows, there's no pedestrian access. He had lost his wallet so he sat in the morgue for three days until my mother reported him missing. I was seven.'

'Oh Johan.' I put my arms around him, feeling helpless. He hugged me back, but he didn't quite melt into me, the tension in his spine holding him back. It crossed my mind that it must be lonely being such a big guy. I loved it when we snuggled on the couch and I sat between his legs, wrapped in his arms, completely encapsulated by him. It didn't seem fair I couldn't do the same to him.

'It is fine,' he said finally, pulling back. He wiped his eyes with the back of his hand. 'It is life. I just hoped I would not turn out to be so much his son.'

'You're not, though,' I said firmly. 'For one thing, you're not nearly as bad, and more importantly, you're getting help. That makes all the difference. That makes you brave, and brilliant, and — I'm really proud of you.'

'I think the curry is ready.'

'Then I am proud of you and also hungry.'

He laughed and I carried our wine to the little table in the living room while he dished up.

After we'd eaten the truly spectacular meal and I'd moaned and groaned and held my stomach in ecstasy, going way over the top to make him laugh, we sat at the table for a while. My feet were in his lap and he was rubbing them absentmindedly as I poured the last of the red into our glasses. The candles on the table were the only light in the room, and it was almost dark outside. The candlelight flickered over Johan's face as he smiled over at me.

He looked so warm and kind and *Johan* that a part of me wanted to take a picture, march right over to that shitty club and shove it in Linda Andersson's face then punch her lights out.

Not that I had the first clue of how a person punches

someone's lights out, I didn't even have siblings to practice on. The only person I'd ever tried to whack was a guy who felt me up on Trafalgar Square at midnight on New Year's Eve once upon a time. I'd whirled around and swung for him, but had only succeeded in sort of thumping his shoulder and as he was wearing a thick puffa jacket I'd might as well have punched a pillow. It was frankly embarrassing for both of us, though I felt a bit better after I'd emptied a bottle of Smirnoff Ice on his head.

Maybe I should empty a bottle of Smirnoff Ice on Linda Andersson's head.

'I love you,' Johan said, and little fireworks of joy exploded deep inside me. I shifted my foot, and grinned as I heard his breath catch in his throat. I started to massage with my toes. He ran his hand lightly up my other calf, stroking that little sensitive spot behind my knee and I gasped, started to move my toes faster. He muttered something breathlessly in Swedish and I grinned, because I always loved the moment all his English flew out of his head.

I slipped off my seat and straddled him, replacing my toes with my hips as he gripped my arse. I kissed him deeply, felt his fingers fumble under my shirt and run lightly over my tummy as my tongue found his. He slid the fabric of my bra aside with his thumb and I moaned.

And then there was a bang at the door.

'Ignore it,' I whispered, slipping my hand between us to undo his jeans.

The banging continued, loud, urgent.

'Fuu-uck,' he muttered. His English was back.

I sighed in frustration and got up, smoothing my skirt and straightening my bra as Johan answered the door.

It was Liv. She tossed the briefest smile in my direction

as she unleashed a flow of rapid Swedish at Johan, and I mentally added 'sense of timing' to the list of things I didn't like about her. Johan led her over to the sofa with an apologetic look at me, as I cleared the table with a couple more bangs and crashes than were strictly necessary.

19

'Oh my god I would have strangled her with my bare hands,' Maddie laughed the next day as I wound up my tirade on Liv's general awfulness with the finale of her interruption the night before.

'She's lucky I didn't.'

We were in a gym in a part of Stockholm I'd never been to before. When I'd realised it was near where Maddie lived with her girlfriend Lena, I'd texted to see if she fancied a workout. It was one of those fancy places that smelled more of new equipment than sweat. The upbeat house music that pounded from the speakers was presumably cutting edge and the whole place was a bit suspiciously *Instagrammable* and gleaming for my tastes. Not, to be fair, that there technically exists a gym that's to my taste, on account of them being places where one goes to exercise.

Maddie turned out to be one of those bonkers keen fit people though, which I should have been prepared for, what with her being Australian and all. She was now lying on a mat, raising and lowering her legs, and I was sitting next to her, mucking about with the smallest weights I could find, which I figured at least showed willing.

'What did she even want that late at night?' Maddie asked.

'Johan said later it was some kind of boy trouble, though she seemed more irritated than upset if you ask me. 'Course, she always seems irritated to me. Maybe that's just her face.'

Maddie chuckled and rolled over, started raising her shoulders like a fish on dry land.

'It was more the fact that it's a one room flat, for heaven's sake, what exactly did she expect me to do with myself? I did the dishes as slowly as I could, but then it was a choice between sitting on the kitchen floor, or going back to the main room with them and pretending to be invisible. I ended up sort of perching at the edge of the bed reading a magazine, wishing I had noise cancelling earphones.'

In truth I'd sat staring blindly at the magazine, composing and discarding several scathing comments in my head as I watched them out the corner of my eye and tried to telepathically transmit orders to her to stop bloody touching his bloody arm.

'It's your flat too,' said Maddie, 'she shouldn't make you feel like that. They could have gone out for a drink if she didn't want to include you, but however you look at it, it was rude. I wouldn't stand for one of Lena's friends behaving like that, and we've at least got a separate bedroom. I mean, there's Swedish shyness and there is plain being an arsehole. Ignoring you like that in your own home is just plain being an arsehole.'

Maddie got up and went over to some kind of metal torture device. I perched on a bench nearby, toying with my pointless teensy dumbbells. I felt better already. There's something about pouring it all out to a friend, repackaging the whole thing into a funny story, that took the sting out a bit I should have taken Maddie up on her offer of a coffee ages ago.

'Did Johan apologise at least?'

I shrugged. 'Not really. He's — he's so amazing and sensitive most of the time, but it's like he's got this blind spot where his friends are concerned. They've all known each other forever, I don't think he can imagine what it's like to be on the outside of them any more, you know?'

Maddie nodded. 'I've got a mate like that at home. Our mums were best friends and we were born within a couple of months of each other so we've known each other our whole lives. Over the years a few people have pointed out she's a bit weird. She isn't rude exactly, she's just off in her own world a lot of the time, but I'm so used to it I don't even notice.'

'Yeah, I think it's something like that. There's also —' I hesitated, not sure whether I wanted to get into the rest of it. It wasn't that it was a secret as such, just that dropping *so I found this dead body that turned out to be my boyfriend's ex and half the city think he murdered her* into conversation is harder than you'd think. 'There's other stuff that's been going on, and that little crew have really supported Johan a lot. I think he thinks he owes them.'

Maddie finished her set and took a swig of water.

'So what are we actually doing here, babe?' she asked.

'I believe it's known as exercising?'

She shook her head. 'Yeah I am, but you're mucking about like you're trying to get out of gym class at school. Which is totally fine, I don't give a crap if you work out or not, I'm just wondering why we're here?'

I shrugged. I took a sip of water, though she was entirely correct that I hadn't sweated a drop yet.

'Is it something to do with the hot trainer dude you keep looking over at? Are you cheating on Johan? Or trying to? It's totally cool by me, it's just that if I'm accessory to a spot of stalking, I like to know it.'

Over in the far corner where the big scary weights and grunting men lived, Gustav Lindström was encouraging a client through a gruelling set of what I believe are called back squats. Whatever they were, they did not look a lot of fun.

'I'm not cheating on Johan,' I began carefully. 'Or trying to, either.'

'But we are here because of Mr Muscle over there.'

'I'd like to talk to him.'

'Because —?'

'Because — because I think Johan's last girlfriend might have been about to dump Johan for him when she was murdered.'

'Okay,' said Maddie. 'I think I need a juice.'

In the juice bar, I picked at a raw muffin and poured out the whole story, while Maddie sipped something that looked like pond scum. When I was finally finished, she sat quietly for a few moments. In the testosterone corner, Gustav's client was roaring as he deadlifted what appeared to be the weight of a small horse.

'Holy shit, babe, I would have been on the first plane home.' She reached over and squeezed my hand. 'You're a fucking warrior.'

'I was hardly going to leave Johan. And I don't think you'd leave Lena in the lurch like that either.'

Maddie grinned and shrugged. 'She could come with me I guess.'

I laughed and shoved away the thought that Johan might not follow me if I announced I was off. I mean, of course he would, it was just that when I thought about it, I couldn't remember him moving to London being discussed as an option. Which would actually make a lot more sense, given that his job was a bit more easily transferrable, and he could already speak English. Not that I would have wanted him to move, I was definitely up for the adventure of a new life. We probably did talk about it and I dismissed the idea so quickly I'd forgotten.

'But all that stuff we talk about at the newcomers coffee,' Maddie was saying, 'all those little things you have to figure out, learn the language, deal with new people all the time, take numbers to queue — hell, gender neutral toilets gave me the heebie jeebies for months. Washing your hands next to some bloke, it's *weird*,' she grinned. 'Until you get so used to it that you go home for Christmas and nearly get beaten up in a bar in Brisbane for absentmindedly following a guy into the gents'. The point is, all that normal immigrant shit is more than enough do your head in. And you've had this on top of it. I'd be a wreck.'

'Meh, I'm tough as old boots,' I said with a smile that was a bit more wobbly than I'd intended. Maddie reached over and squeezed my hand.

'Okay,' she said slowly. 'The police are still investigating?'

'I guess. There's apparently some law about early investigations being top secret, so we don't really know what they're up to.'

'But his lawyer doesn't reckon they're closing in on him or anything?'

'He's innocent.'

'Yeah I get that, but rightly or wrongly, he's not in any danger right now?'

'I suppose not.'

'So what are you doing all this for, babe? Isn't it best to let the police get on with their jobs, then deal with whatever happens? If he's innocent, you've got nothing to worry about, right?'

I shook my head. 'Even if they don't charge him in the end, he'll have it hanging over his head for the rest of his life — like that Linda said, people will think he got away with it unless they catch someone else.'

'And do you think that guy killed her?' Maddie nodded in Gustav's direction.

'I don't know. But if she was seeing him in the days or weeks before her death, then he is potentially relevant. He might know something, he might not, but I have to talk to him.'

Maddie wrinkled her nose as Gustav and his client walked by, both of them essentially more gorilla than man. 'You need to be careful Ellie.'

'I'm hardly going to approach him alone in the dark or anything.'

'That's not what I mean. Though yeah, he could break your neck with his thumb, so watch out on that front too, but — Lena is police. She works with domestic abuse cases, so she won't know anything about any of this, but I do know from her that they don't fuck about here. The laws are seriously strict. There's no bail, did you know that? If they arrest someone, it means they've got a case so airtight it could you could travel to the bottom of the sea in it. If you're going to step on Swedish police's toes, you need to be really, really careful. For your own sake.'

'I know what I'm doing.'

'In London you do.'

Her gaze was unrelenting. I looked down at my juice.

'Plus, surely when you investigate a story, you're not invested in the outcome, are you? Isn't that the whole point, to be neutral?'

I nodded.

'But you're not neutral here, are you? You're trying to prove Johan is innocent — and what if you can't?'

'He didn't kill her.'

Maddie put her hands up in surrender. 'No, I know, I'm not saying that. But, what's that thing about how you can't prove a negative? What if it turns out to be most likely a tragic accident, but there's no real way to prove it? Real life can be messy like that. How will you handle it if —'

'There is proof,' I said, draining my carrot and apple juice, which hadn't been nearly as disgusting as I had expected. I turned away from the concern in Maddie's eyes. 'I just have to find it.'

HALF AN HOUR LATER, Maddie had gone home, I had stretched more than was possibly good for a person, and Gustav Lindström was finally done with his client. They parted with much backslapping and self satisfied laughter, and as he turned towards the reception bit, I darted after him.

'Excuse me? Oh sorry — do you speak English? *Engelska?*'

'Yes of course,' he said coldly.

'Great, thank you. I'm — I just saw you, with your client, and I wondered if you had any, umm, vacancies? Is that what it's called? I mean, could you — work me out?'

He looked me up and down as though I were a prize calf. 'You want to lose weight?'

Fuck you, and the horse you rode in on, I thought, then quickly swallowed that and forced a smile.

'A bit, maybe. I mostly want to get, you know —' I belatedly realised I was making a muscle like *Popeye*. 'Strong,' I finished lamely. 'Stronger, at any rate.'

'Are you willing to commit?'

'Sure!'

'I mean, seriously.'

'Umm, sure?'

'You will train when I tell you, for how long I tell you and how hard I tell you?'

'That sounds as though it would be the point.'

'You eat exactly what I tell you? Sleep when I tell you?'

Was this guy serious? I got a sudden vision of him standing over me and Johan in bed, commanding us to sleep, and I bit down a giggle. 'I mean, as long as there's nothing good on telly.'

'You don't want to train,' he said dismissively. 'What do you want?'

'Like I said, I want muscles. One or two, at least.'

With an impatient smirk, he started to walk down the corridor. I scuttled after him.

'I want to ask you about Sanna Johansson.'

'Go to hell.'

'If I could just ask a question or two first?'

'Are you a journalist?'

I hesitated. 'That's not why I want to talk to you.'

'Go to hell, journalist scum.'

He flung open the door of the men's changing rooms.

'I know you loved her,' I blurted desperately.

He froze.

'I think she loved you too. Doesn't she deserve the truth to come out?'

He hesitated a moment and I held my breath, then he stepped into the men's changing room and slammed the door behind him.

Bugger.

20

I just want to know what happened. I'm not angry, I'm not bitter — I don't feel anything any more. I'm numb, I think. I'm trying to move on, trying to find some kind of peace. But I can't do that until I know. There can be no peace for me while I have these questions.

I won't tell the police anything, I won't tell anyone. I suppose you have no reason to trust that is the truth, but if you look into my eyes you will see someone who is broken. I'm not on a mission of vengeance or justice. Not anymore. I doubt anyone would believe me at this point anyway.

They think I'm crazy. The police. My friends. His family. My family. They think I've gone mad with grief, like a character in a gothic novel. They expect me to start wearing my wedding dress to work, or wander the streets cradling dolls instead of the babies I'll never have.

Maybe I will. Maybe I should just give into it. Maybe that is who I am now.

So that's why I'm not any threat. Whatever you tell me, there's nothing I can do with the information even if I wanted to.

They would listen patiently and send me home, even if I tried to tell them. I'm no longer someone people listen to. I'm barely even a person any more. They think I'm going crazy because I lost him. But it's not even him any more. I am crazy because I lost me.

You are the only person who can give me back.

21

I 've gone soft, I thought later that evening. I sighed in frustration and Johan looked up from the football game on TV. It had been years since I'd fucked up a doorstepping that spectacularly. Doorstepping — approaching an interviewée cold, most often on their own doorstep — was my thing. I was brilliant at it.

People have become more suspicious of press in recent years, but at the end of the day, everyone wants their side of the story out. All you need to do is work out what it is they're desperate for you to tell the world, and promise to do it. Shout it louder than the rest, and you'll be ushered inside, giving a triumphant finger to the rest of the press gaggle as the door closes behind you. Works every time.

Johan was slouched on the sofa, beer in hand. He'd barely spoken a word since I got home, though he'd been texting the whole time. Presumably discussing the game with Krister, though what on earth it was people found to actually discuss about a bunch of blokes kicking a ball at one another, I would never know. *The ball went that way, then it went the other! Someone kicked it — yes, with his foot!*

I was curled up on the bed with my laptop, scrolling through Gustav Lindström's irritatingly locked down Facebook profile. He might not post often anyway, I told myself, clicking through the handful of photos that were public. But there were posts, tantalisingly invisible to me, I was sure of it.

Sanna had liked two of his photos. She'd be able to see his whole profile, I thought sourly, clicking back and forth between her profile and his.

Johan roared and I jumped a mile. Hammarby had scored. Hammar-*bai*, I mentally corrected myself, remembering again the way Liv had curled up on the couch — my couch — like she bloody lived here, staring into my boyfriend's eyes as she unloaded her troubles on him as though I didn't exist.

Maddie was right. She'd been lucky I hadn't lamped her one.

Of course it wasn't exactly likely Gustav Lindström had posted anything obviously incriminating on his Facebook wall. I was looking for connections between him and Sanna that might shed some more light what they were to one another. Mutual friends, mutual likes or events. Photos with glimpses of body language. Their relationship, whatever it was, was a crucial piece of the jigsaw puzzle. I was certain of it.

Of course, once upon a time I was also certain that the Guardian news desk job I'd applied for was mine, that Dan Philipson absolutely fancied me back, and that my then flatmate wasn't going to abscond with her half of the rent. It wasn't exactly unheard of for my gut to tell me a load of old bollocks, I thought with a sigh. Johan yelled at the TV and I went into the kitchen for a cup of tea.

For all I knew, I thought as the kettle boiled, there was

something posted on Gustav's wall that gave him an alibi for the weekend Sanna disappeared. He could have been on holiday on the other side of the world, with another woman.

Another woman. A thought burrowed its way into my brain and I hesitated, knowing it meant playing with fire. It might not work. He might just ignore a friend request from someone he didn't know. But if so, then no harm, no foul. It couldn't be traced back to me in any case.

I brought my cup of tea back into the living room. Almost before I knew what I was doing, I'd logged out of my Facebook account and created a new one using the dummy email address I sometimes used to communicate with witnesses. I called her Agneta, after the blonde one in ABBA, the first Swedes I'd known and loved.

So as not to involve some poor anonymous woman off Google images, I used a photo of me. Not one Gustav would ever recognise as the bird who approached him that afternoon; my mum barely recognised me in this picture. It was from the height of my club days, the only photographic evidence I'd allowed to survive.

My diet of toast and cocaine had rendered me pretty much skin and bone, my cheekbones hollow in a way I'd hoped made me look like Kate Moss, but in fact more accurately resembled Skeletor. One morning, in a fit of manic come down, I'd bleached my hair straw-white. Or, tried to. Using actual bleach meant for cleaning the toilet. I still had some scars on the back of my neck from the burns, and it's a miracle I hadn't got any on my face or in my eyes. Looking like Worzel Gummidge (meets Skeletor: hot, eh?) for a few months was actually pretty good going for having not-entirely-on-purpose doused myself in bleach.

The point was, I didn't look like myself. To be on the safe side, I made the image black and white and blurred it by 1%, which obscured my features just a teensy bit more, and would probably be taken for arty-fartiness. I clicked on the page of the gym where Gustav worked, and sent a handful of friend requests to people who had liked their most recent few posts, then with the help of Google translate, posted in Swedish: *back on Facebook guys - sorry for being dramatic!* followed by a row of the embarrassed face emoji. That would hopefully take care of my lack of previous activity.

Once seven randoms had agreed to be friends with Agneta, I took a deep breath and requested Gustav.

22

T he bar was definitely not what I was expecting. It was in a cellar, a few blocks from Johan's flat, which you accessed by a narrow, metal spiral staircase that I imagined must be a Health and Safety nightmare when mixed with alcohol. Downstairs, the place was cavernous, with bar area leading to games area leading to more bars, seemingly forever, exposed concrete walls and pipes randomly strewn with fairy lights and garlands of plastic flowers.

The air was filled with thwacks and cracks and shouts of laughter from the various air hockey games, bowling alleys and huge industrial tables crowded with chattering groups of friends. It wasn't the sort of place one could sit unobtrusively alone with a beer and a book, but on the other hand, I was confident I could wander pretending to look for toilets or my friends, more or less indefinitely. I hovered near some kind of mass ping pong game, a group of teenagers marching around the table handing the bats smoothly to the next person without missing a beat, my eyes flicking over every table in search of Gustav.

He'd checked in here not fifteen minutes ago. Possibly a

couple of beers had helped his decision to accept Agneta the sexy Skeletor's friend request, though the fact he turned out to have 3427 friends suggested he wasn't exactly discerning. A quick skim through his profile hadn't turned up much that pinged interesting before his check-in just a few blocks away proved irresistible.

I wasn't going to approach him again. Two attempts in a matter of hours would get me nowhere. I just wanted to — see him, I suppose. In the wild. Glance over who he was with — possibly someone I would recognise from the memorial, or Sanna's friends list.

Linda Andersson had turned out to be one of his 3427 friends, which might be nothing or might explain why she'd taken such an anti-Johan stance. They could be drinking together. He could be on a date. There had been no obvious sign of a girlfriend on his profile, but it wasn't uncommon for a certain kind of guy to fail to advertise on social media that they were spoken for.

'Hey Ellie!' I jumped a mile, then hastily composed my features into a smile as Mia gave me a hug. 'What are you doing here? Where is Johan?'

'Oh, he's not here, I'm meeting a group of other new immigrants,' I said, glancing around as though this group might magically appear. That was the story I'd given Johan too.

'Oh fun, so great you are getting to know people. I am glad.'

'Yeah, I'm just, uhh — hoping I've got the right place. I didn't realise it would be so big.'

'Well have a drink with me first anyway,' she said, slipping her arm through mine and dragging me towards one of the bars. 'My friend is late, and we haven't had a chance to talk properly in ages.'

Mia was really alright, I thought a little while later as she poured the last of our bottle of rosé into my glass.

'Did you know that Johan and I were once engaged?' she'd asked as soon as we sat down, and I'm not entirely proud of the fact that my heart lurched.

She laughed. 'On our first day of school, the teacher asked me to help Johan and Krister to tie their shoes. Krister told me he could do it himself, but I helped Johan, then I informed him that I thought we should now get married and he agreed. After recess, I decided I had changed my mind, and he also agreed. My first great love story. *Skål.*' She raised her glass to mine and took a sip.

'I read somewhere that you should thank all the previous girlfriends of the man you end up with, because they put in the training you benefit from,' I smiled, taking a gulp of my wine. Some games machine started beeping frantically and a few people cheered. 'I don't know any of the others, so I guess I'll thank you.'

Mia's smile froze for an instant and I could have kicked myself. Sanna. Technically I hadn't known her, but still.

'I'm sorry,' I said, and Mia smiled, shook her head.

'Don't be silly. We can't all live our lives on, what is it — tender —?'

'Tenterhooks,' I supplied.

'Yes. Sanna is dead and that is terrible, but we are not and we must live.'

'I think Johan told me the story about the shoelaces,' I said quickly, trying to change the subject. 'It rings a bell. Though he conveniently left out his first engagement. I was shocked he didn't already know how to tie his own laces at seven years old.'

'Things were a little bit difficult for him at home when he was a child. I don't think his mother had so much time to teach him that sort of thing. I'm sorry, maybe he hasn't told you —'

'He has. I should have made the connection' I said, a prickly feeling dancing down my spine. That little flinch back on the jetty where we were waiting for Krister and I'd called him a plank. He hadn't been ready to tell me, didn't know if he could trust me yet.

She nodded. 'I'm pleased he told you. He must really trust you.'

'Lucky he has such good friends as you guys. You've obviously been there for him a lot over the years.'

'We are lucky, also,' Mia replied.

'Did you know Sanna well?' I asked. 'Johan said you worked together.'

'Not really. Our paths crossed sometimes, but we were not close friends. She always seemed fun, but — I'm not sure. Have you ever read the F Scott Fitzgerald quotation, *hedonism is but despair turned inside out*? Sometimes Sanna made me think of it. She had a little bit of darkness in her.'

'Don't we all?'

Mia looked surprised. 'Do you?'

I shrugged. 'I suppose so. I think everyone does, given the right circumstances. I think people are generally more complicated than we often give them credit for.'

'Hmm.' Mia refilled our glasses as she thought this over. 'I always wondered if — if what happened to her was not an accident.'

'Do you mean suicide?'

'Perhaps. Perhaps a cry for help that went too far. She was very upset that day.'

'Because of the argument with Johan?'

Mia went quiet a moment. I caught myself holding my breath. 'I am not sure,' she said finally, 'but I did not believe they were healthy together. It was — what do you call it — a toxic relationship. They were two good people who were very bad for each other. The way he talked to her sometimes — it was not the Johan I know.'

A little chill danced down my spine. Behind us, the group of teenagers cheered as someone won the ping pong relay. I took a sip of my wine.

'Some relationships are like that,' I said. 'Did you see her get in the kayak that day?'

Mia shook her head. 'Krister and I had gone swimming. There is another island you can swim to, and we sat over on that beach for a little while before we swam back.'

So Johan and Liv were on the island alone when Sanna disappeared, I thought, an iciness sliding into my veins.

'Johan said he was relieved when he woke up and found her gone.'

'I am not so surprised,' Mia said, her eyes troubled.

'He would never —'

'Of course not,' Mia said quickly. 'I don't think he even knew she had the pills with her.'

'They were hers?'

Mia nodded. 'She had a prescription. She was supposed to use them for fear of flying only, but that weekend she told me that she took half of one sometimes when things got a little bit too much.'

'Did you tell the police this?'

'Of course. They had discovered already it was her prescription.'

So the rumour about Johan having access to the drugs because he was a nurse was absolute bollocks. I smiled at Mia.

'Maybe the police will officially declare it suicide,' I said.

'God, that's a horrible thing to hope for, but at least Johan won't be living under the shadow of it any more.'

'There is nothing wrong in hoping for the truth,' Mia said quietly.

'That poor girl.' I raised my glass, though there was only the dregs left in it. 'To Sanna.'

Mia took a sip, but she didn't meet my eye.

'Are you guys going to get on with planning your wedding now?' I asked, and Mia rolled her eyes.

'Oh my god, I wish someone had told me how boring wedding stuff was,' she grinned. 'I keep trying to persuade Krister to elope but he is determined to be a blushing bride.'

She rolled her eyes and I laughed and decided that Mia and I could definitely be friends.

23

Another bottle of wine later, I was distinctly wobbly as I hugged Mia goodbye on the corner. She didn't appear to be nearly as pissed as I was, which I remembered from Midsummer as well. She must be one of those bizarre specimens that could hold her alcohol. I'd try not to hold it against her.

I had stumbled into the little square with the fountain and tripped over my own feet on the gravel pathway before I noticed that I'd taken a wrong turn somewhere. Or rather, I had failed to turn left wherever it was I should have. It was almost full dark, and it took me a few moments to get my bearings.

The fountain was off at this time of night, and I was more than a little concerned I would end up tripping into it if I wasn't careful. Only I could get myself lost in a park the size of a postage stamp, I thought crossly, half picturing Johan's expression if I phoned him to rescue me from the middle of the fountain. I felt weirdly disoriented and way drunker than I ought to be.

Just as I remembered that I'd forgotten to have dinner so

was in fact precisely as drunk as I ought to be, the world fell out from under my feet and I went flying onto the grass. With a grunt I rolled over, trying to figure out what in the hell I'd managed to trip over, when I felt another blow to my ribs that sent me reeling.

'What the fuck,' I shouted, scrabbling to my feet as a huge, shadowy dude came into focus.

Gustav Lindström.

'What do you want?' he spat, and something about his expression made my stomach twist in terror. I glanced around. We were in the middle of the city. Dozens of apartments overlooked the square, there had to be other people wandering home from late night drinks, dog walkers. Surely. Somewhere.

'Nothing —' I said quietly, taking a step back, my hands in front of me in surrender. 'Absolutely nothing. I'm just going home after a drink with my friend.'

'You followed me. I told you I don't want to talk to you.'

'And I respect that. It's a small city. We just happened to run into each other.' I was amazed at how steady my voice sounded. 'I'm sorry to have bothered you, I'll just be on my way —'

'How do you know Sanna loved me?'

Before I could answer he staggered off, puked in a nearby bin. I hesitated a moment, wondering if I should scarper, then I grabbed a bottle of water from my bag and followed him over, handed it to him.

'You really loved her?' I asked gently. He sank to his knees, still clutching onto the bin. I crouched next to him as he nodded miserably.

'For many years,' he muttered, leaning his forehead against the bin.

'What happened?'

'It was all my fault. I fucked it all up, so many times.'

He took several deep breaths. The night was still, and for a few moments the only sound was his jagged breathing until a dog yapped from somewhere nearby and I breathed a tiny sigh of relief.

'You were quite young when you got together?' I asked finally.

He nodded miserably, lost in thought. I waited.

'I thought I was supposed to have a different girl every night,' he muttered finally. 'Thought I would regret it if I didn't.' He gave a shaky sigh. 'I didn't even realise I already had the only girl I wanted.'

I slipped my hand into my bag, felt around for my phone. Gustav was still leaning against the bin. I prayed he wouldn't notice the glow as I swiped to open it, tapped the voice recorder app.

'Did Sanna break it off with you?'

'We could never stay apart for long. On and off, is that what you say? We were on and off and on and off, until she met him.'

A shadow crossed his expression, and it was there again. That tiny whisper of real menace that made me glad I was crouching and not sitting. I shifted my weight a little on my feet, ready to dart away if I needed to.

'You mean Johan?'

'The nurse?' he spat. 'The fucking nurse. *He is a grown up, he knows how to be in a real relationship.* What does that even mean? I loved her.'

'Did you try to tell her that?'

'She was just using him, trying to make me jealous. She didn't love him. Didn't really want him. She wanted me.'

'So you tried to talk to her?'

'I took the boat.'

My heart lurched. He took a boat that weekend? To the island? I glanced at my phone to make sure it was recording.

'I had to tell her. She had to understand what she meant to me.'

'Did you see her that weekend?'

'I just wanted to say that I loved her. That it would be different this time. I didn't want any other girls any more, I just wanted her.'

'I bet she was happy to hear that,' I said softly.

He didn't reply, and after a moment I realised his shoulders were shaking with silent sobs.

'Did you get to the island? Did you find her?'

He turned around, sat with his back leaning against the bin, his head lolling to one side as he muttered under his breath. 'She said she was happy with the nurse. She told me to leave her alone.'

'Then what happened?'

'She was so beautiful. I loved her so much. How could she chose him?'

'What did you do Gustav? How did Sanna die?'

He didn't respond. I waited, barely daring to breathe until I heard him snore. He was out for the count. I propped the bottle of water next to him and I left.

24

'It's not a confession.'

Maddie's girlfriend Lena had dark brown hair cut in a blunt bob, and a serious gaze that made her a tiny bit intimidating even as she sat crosslegged at the kitchen table in her pyjamas and a hoodie. We were sitting opposite each other as Maddie made coffee. I'd apologised all over the place for the late hour when I all but tumbled in their front door a few minutes earlier but they swore they had still been up.

'But he says he went to talk to her that weekend.'

'No, he says he wanted to talk to her. You say it was that weekend.'

'He took a boat. He must have been going to an island.'

'Stockholm is made up of many islands.'

'But —'

Maddie brought coffees and a plate of homemade biscuits to the table.

'He needs to be interrogated properly. He is drunk and your recording would not be admissible in any investigation without context or a witness. You are not incorrect that the police will be interested to talk to him based on this, but no more than that. It could be something, or it could be a wasted, broken hearted guy talking shit.'

'But it could be something,' I muttered stubbornly.

Lena smiled briefly. 'It could be something. One thing that surprises me is that he does not refer to the police having spoken to him already — he didn't say that when you approached him at the gym either, did he?'

I shook my head.

'I wonder if he has been missed by the investigation. How did you identify him?'

'Facebook. He posted on her wall *Fy fan, Sanna* the other day, and it struck me as an intense thing to say to another guy's girlfriend. Then when Linda Andersson said Sanna might have been leaving Johan for someone else, I put two and two together.'

'Nice work.'

'Especially if it turns out he was there that weekend.'

Lena nodded slowly. 'Or it could be that an ex who would not give up added to the stress Mia was talking about. It could have pushed her over the edge.'

'I've been thinking about these rumours about Johan,' I said. 'The fact that a newspaper picked it up in the first place and the whole world instantly declared him guilty — doesn't it feel a bit, I don't know, deliberate? Especially given that the police haven't even confirmed foul play. Like, whatever happened, Johan is already guilty. End of story.

'And more than that,' I persisted, seeing doubt leap into Lena's eyes, 'if the story was about him having a hot temper that possibly got out of control, I could buy that people had heard things based in reality but twisted by gossip. But the way Linda described him, he sounded cold, cruel even. It's so far off the mark that I can't believe it's based on anything real.'

'Then what could it be?' asked Maddie.

'Well what if it's not just gossip, but rumours that have been deliberately planted?' I said. 'What if it suits someone to have people think badly of Johan — to suspect him if they're going to suspect anyone?'

'Do you believe Gustav Lindström is capable of such manipulation?' Lena asked.

'I don't know. Maybe.'

'It is possible also, that you are considering the story only through the eyes of protecting Johan,' Lena said gently. 'I read newspapers, I talk to people about things happening in the city every day, and I have never heard of this story, much less believe Johan to be guilty. It could be that it seems to him the entire world suspects him, but I am not so sure it is the case.'

'But it is possible Gustav spread these rumours,' I persisted. 'He knows all the same people that Sanna did, and he's at least Facebook friends with Linda Andersson.'

'Isn't it odd then, that this Linda didn't know it was Sanna's ex she was thinking of leaving Johan for?' Maddie pointed out. 'She just said it was some other guy, right?'

'Maybe she knew and just didn't say so to me?'

'Maybe.'

I sighed. Maybe not. Every time I thought I was on to something, it was as though a fog rolled in and obscured it all again. My mind kept flashing back to the look Gustav had given me barely an hour earlier in that dark little park. There had been menace in his eyes. I thought of Sanna's kayak floating upside down in the freezing water, and I shuddered.

'I've been getting the impression that Sanna was secretive,' I said slowly. 'Or perhaps distant is the right word, she kept herself to herself. I don't feel as though many people knew her particularly well. On one hand people describe her as this wild party girl, but there's not masses of evidence of that. Most of her friends' Facebooks and Instagrams are filled with pictures of mad, drunken nights, but hers is a good bit more reserved. A handful of thoughtful posts about politics, very few photos at all. Then there's what Mia said about her being troubled, or even depressed.' I shrugged. 'All those things aren't mutually exclusive, exactly, but she is a bit of an enigma.'

'So she could have other secrets you've not come across at all yet.' said Maddie.

'I suppose she could.'

'I think that you should go to the police, tell them about your conversation with Gustav,' Lena said. 'Don't admit you recorded it. unless they specifically ask, it could confuse matters. Just tell them what he said to you and let them take it from there. And then I think you should drop this matter and let the police take care of it. That is my advice.'

I nodded, feeling exhausted suddenly. She was right. I'd bitten off more than I could chew.

'If I were you I'd nip home for a bit too,' said Maddie. 'Just a couple of days even, give yourself a break. Breathe in some smelly London air and gorge yourself on your mum's home cooking, you know? Charge yourself up. Whatever happens with all this, if Johan is going to start therapy, he's going to need you firing on all sixes, babe.'

I nodded. The thought of sitting on a minging tube, rattling away beneath London on the way to my mum's brought a lump to my throat and for a second I was tempted to phone a taxi direct for the airport then and there. 'Yeah, might do. Just for the weekend or something.'

'Bring me back some Fruit Pastilles if you do.'

'Deal.'

25

It was Lena's job to be measured and cautious, I thought as the bus trundled back towards Södermalm a little while later. She had to refrain from coming down on any one side until the evidence was conclusive, but she hadn't been there. She hadn't seen the look in Gustav's eye.

It was dark and silent when I got off the bus at Åsögatan, and there was a chill in the air that seemed to reach my bones. As I trudged the couple of blocks to Johan's flat, all I could think of was climbing into our warm bed and drifting off into a long, deep, sleep. I may or may not go to London, I thought. Maybe I should focus properly on my Swedish life instead. Look to the future. Sign up for Swedish for Immigrants classes, do something about finding some work. The bottom of my bank account was beckoning.

When I turned the corner into Johan's road, I spotted a car sitting outside the building, and my heart started to thud. It was just a plain, dark coloured sedan, but instantly I knew it spelt trouble. For a mad instant I considered turning and running.

'Ellie James?'

I blinked, confused. It was them. The detectives, the dark haired woman and the rockstar guy. The ones I was going to phone first thing in the morning. Did they know? Had Lena contacted them?

'We would like you to come with us, please,' said the woman, with a pleasant, but formal, smile.

'What — why? Is Johan okay?' I stammered.

'He is fine,' the guy said, in a lilting accent Johan had explained meant he came from the north of Sweden.

'Then why? What do you want?'

'Did you argue with Gustav Lindström earlier this evening?'

'Argue?' I looked from one to the other, but their faces were impassive. 'No, I wouldn't call it that. We spoke. Why?'

'A witness claimed he knocked you to the ground.'

'I fell over, but I'm not even certain — we were both drunk, it was dark. What is this about?'

'And did you leave him unconscious?'

'Yeah, he passed out. I left my bottle of water next to him. He was snoring.'

'He was alive?'

'I beg your pardon?'

'One hour ago Gustav Lindström was found dead at Nytorget.'

Her voice sounded distorted over the roaring of blood in my ears. I stared at her in shock. My breath caught in my throat as horror fluttered through me.

'He — I mean, he was sitting up, I never even thought there was a chance he would choke or anything.'

The rockstar guy opened the car door. 'We would like you to come with us now, please.'

26

'A heart attack?'

I stared at the two detectives. The rockstar guy, who had introduced himself as Henrik, made a note on his pad, while the woman, Nadja, stared at me.

'I don't understand, he's Mr Fitness, how could —' Then I cut myself off as I thought of his unnaturally bulging muscles, the tight neck that looked as though it must ache. 'Steroids?' I asked.

'Not according to his brother, who we spoke to earlier,' Henrik replied. 'Though the tests for drugs in his system are not yet complete.'

I nodded, trying to slow my breathing a bit. My heart was hammering in my chest. I couldn't quite get my head around what was happening. One minute I was about to climb into bed and snuggle up to Johan's warm back, and the next I was sitting here in this chilly interrogation room, discussing the death of a man I had spoken to just a couple of hours ago. I could see Gustav Lindström clearly in my mind's eye, slumped against the rubbish bin, slurring about how much he loved Sanna. And now he was dead. It wouldn't quite sink in, as though I could sense the reality of it, but every time I tried to grasp it, it flickered just out of reach. The word *dead* rattled around my head, echoing and meaningless.

I took a sip of a coffee that had long gone cold. I've never been in a police interrogation room before, but I've always imagined them pretty rank. Dimly lit, covered in graffiti, probably stinking of piss. Possibly with one of those little high up barred windows, so that streetlights from outside cast shadows of bars across the accused's face, making them feel as though they were already in prison.

My impressions may have been formed more than a bit by telly.

Either way, this room was nothing like that. Freshly painted in a clean white, it was brightly lit with a pine desk in the centre, surrounded by red plastic chairs. It reminded me of the sort of room in which junior schools might hold parent-teacher conferences. All it needed were a few bits of coloured paper strewn around the walls, covered in messily glued bits of pasta.

They had offered to phone Johan — it turned out they had arrived just as I walked around the corner, so they intercepted me before they got a chance to ring the buzzer — but I declined. He was most likely asleep. I'd fill him in when I got home later, once it was all sorted.

'But surely, a young healthy guy like that — he can't have been much over thirty. Unless he had some sort of pre-existing heart condition?'

'Did he seem to be in any pain or distress when you spoke?' asked Nadja.

'Not physical, other than being pretty wasted. He threw up in the bin.'

'He was in emotional distress?'

'We were talking about his ex girlfriend. Sanna Johansson.'

The two detectives glanced up, exchanged a look. I took a deep breath.

'Sanna Johansson?' repeated Henrik with a frown.

'Look, you know, obviously I found her — what was left of her, a few weeks ago. I know that Johan has been living with the shadow of suspicion over him since she disappeared, and I — I'm a journalist. I'm nosy. It's what I do. I know Johan is innocent, and I have been trying to find proof.'

'Johan is innocent of what?' asked Henrik.

I frowned. 'Of killing Sanna.' I looked from one to the other. They seemed genuinely surprised. 'Didn't you question him in connection with her disappearance?'

'They were in a relationship, of course he was questioned.'

'But then some newspaper got a hold of it. His friends and family have been suspecting him ever since.'

They exchanged another look. 'That is not something we are aware of,' Nadja said carefully.

'Perhaps you had better explain what you have been doing,' added Henrik.

I explained how I had gone to Sanna's memorial, then spoke to Linda Andersson who suggested there was another man in Sanna's life and how that led me to Gustav Lindström. 'He said he talked to Sanna that weekend, the weekend they were away at Krister's island. Or at least he tried to. He said he took his boat out, but she told him she was happy with Johan and to leave her alone.'

'He told you all this tonight?'

'Yes, that's what we were talking about in the little park.'

'Nytorget, where he was found?'

'Yes. He kept saying how much he loved her, how much he regretted screwing things up between them, and that he just wanted her to understand how much he was sorry and wanted her back.'

'And he wanted to tell her this the weekend she disappeared?'

I hesitated. 'He was drunk, talking in circles. It was hard to pin him down exactly. But that was my impression. He specified he had taken a boat to find her, so it stood to reason it was when she was on the island.'

'How exactly did you meet Gustav Lindström tonight?'

'He followed me from the bar. I was there having a drink with a friend.'

That was technically true.

'He must have seen me and came after me when we left. He was quite aggressive to begin with, he sort of crashed into me and I fell over, but when we started talking about Sanna he calmed down. He just seemed broken hearted at that point. Crying about how much he loved her. It don't know if any of it is relevant, but I was planning to contact you first thing tomorrow, for what it's worth.'

The two detectives exchanged a look.

'Sanna Johansson had a restraining order against Gustav Lindström,' said Nadja. 'He had been stalking her in the months following their break up. She did not report that he had been physically violent, but he was extremely possessive and was refusing to accept that they were no longer together.'

'Jealous and insecure,' I said with a frown. 'A woman named Linda Andersson — she worked with Sanna — told me that Sanna's boyfriend was jealous and insecure and she wanted rid of him. I thought she was talking about Johan, but maybe she meant Gustav. She did say he was a nurse, but it's possible she got parts of two stories mixed up.' I looked from one to the other, but their expressions were inscrutable. 'What if she never got in the kayak at all? He could have attacked her then dragged it into the water afterwards to make it look like an accident. You can't know for certain that she drowned.' I swallowed back a shudder. 'There were no lungs left.'

I sat up straighter, suddenly wide awake, my mind racing. 'Maybe the guilt got to him,' I said. 'The stress of her body being found after all these months, the fear that somehow it would be connected back to him. I'm not a doctor, but all that combined with the strain of extreme training, possibly steroids — it's surely possible it could have induced a heart attack.'

The silence was just long enough to make me realise that I had got something very, very wrong. Fear prickled down my spine. I picked up the coffee cup, put it back down again.

'The post mortem examination is still underway,' said Henrik, 'but the coroner noticed one thing at the crime scene. There was a spec of blood on Gustav Lindström's shirt collar, and a puncture mark on his neck.'

'I don't understand.'

'You are correct that the likelihood of a person of his age having a spontaneous heart attack is extremely low, even considering the stress you suggest. It is not impossible, but it is something we must investigate regardless of the circumstances. As we said, the tests to determine drugs in his bloodstream have not yet been completed, but the coroner is of the opinion that Gustav Lindström was injected with a substance that caused a fatal heart attack.'

'What time did you arrive at your friends' apartment

after you left him in the park?' Nadja asked, staring at me intently. My heart started to thud.

'I — uhh, I'm not certain, I didn't pay attention. It was late. Midnight, maybe. Thereabouts.'

'Will your friends vouch for that?'

27

A s I crossed Swedensborgatan next to the train station, I was trembling so deep within me I felt detached from my body. There was a thick, hollow feeling inside me, pressing on my windpipe and it was all I could do to keep breathing as I walked through the darkness. Somebody murdered Gustav Lindström after I left him.

The police thought it could have been me.

The pedestrian walkway opened out, with a wide park bordered by neat trees on my right, a building site to the left. Despite the streetlights it felt pitch black. I scanned the shadows for movement, for any sense that anyone was out there, watching me. Waiting for me.

Of course there bloody wasn't.

I shook myself and walked on briskly, focussing on the lights of Medborgarplatsen ahead. If someone wanted to do me harm, they could have got me hours ago along with Gustav.

The thought wasn't quite as reassuring as I'd hoped.

His killer must have approached within minutes of me leaving. Did they lie in wait, listening to me desperately try to get Gustav to confess? Chuckling to themselves, knowing that Gustav couldn't confess to killing Sanna because they had?

The bars and restaurants around Medborgarplatsen were closed at this time, though the lights of the hot dog kiosk at the far end glowed and the square was bathed in a silvery sheen of street lamps. Suddenly not ready to go home and start explaining to Johan, I sat down on one of the benches, my hands in my pockets. Thoughts were careening around my mind like out of control waltzers. I closed my eyes, trying to focus.

There was something niggling, just out of reach. A thought, something someone had said. Something important, something that didn't quite add up.

The police were going to find my fingerprints and DNA on the water bottle. I'd explained how I left it for him, my words sounding hollow and desperate in my own ears. A witness had seen us argue.

Had I touched him at any point? I suddenly couldn't remember, and chills danced down my spine as I imagined the coroner extracting my skin cells from him and a prison door clanking behind me. I had arrived at Maddie and Lena's at a quarter to twelve. Gustav's body had been found at 1am, and the police believed he had been dead for less than an hour when he was found.

I had an alibi of a quarter of an hour.

But I hadn't killed him. Even if I had the first clue of what drug could induce a heart attack, where would I have got it from? That had to count for something. Whatever the drug was, it wasn't likely to be the sort of thing one might happen to have about their person.

I took a deep breath. They would see that. They had to.

The real killer must have got the drug from somewhere. The real killer must have had reason to kill him.

What would possess me to kill someone I thought could clear Johan?

I knew, though, that motive wasn't nearly as crucial a piece of evidence as TV detective dramas would have you think. Criminal cases live or die on access and opportunity, not airy fairy, forever debatable things like why people do what they do. If the prosecution can prove that the accused acquired the weapon and were in the vicinity, then it's more or less game over — even if no one has a clue what possessed them to murder.

'People are weirder than you think,' a Met Police DCI told me once. 'Some folk just kill because they just do. That don't make for good telly, but it's often how it happens in real life.'

If I wasn't me, I would suspect me right now.

I thought of Gustav Lindström slumped snoring against the bin, tried to imagine reaching into my bag for a syringe, reaching over, injecting his neck, praying that he wouldn't wake before the lethal substance took effect. It was too surreal. It wasn't possible. I was me. How could anyone think I'd killed someone?

That wasn't how it worked, though, I knew that. It might be comforting to imagine the world in terms of goodies and baddies, but I'd been a journalist for too long. I'd reported on the mousy little girl scout leader who'd been sent down for a campaign of astonishing cruelty against Muslim neighbours, the gigantic ex-gangster with a rap sheet a mile long who had almost broken an arm rescuing a kitten from a storm drain. There were no goodies or baddies, there were just people in circumstances.

An icy wind snaked under my collar and I shivered. It was late summer, and there was already a whisper of winter dancing in the air. The cobblestoned square where I sat was wide and dark and empty. All around me, in apartment buildings, people were safe and cosy at home. They slept soundly, buried in well worn duvets, entangled in partners' legs. In the handful of lighted windows dotted here and there, they read, pottered about the kitchen, paced the floor with restless babies.

I sat alone on the bench in the darkness and thought about murder.

Two murders.

The thought slithered into my brain and sparked to life. Two murders, both staged to look like accidents. The first done well enough it went undetected for almost a year. Even now, foul play hadn't been confirmed in Sanna's case.

The other sloppy enough to leave a mark, but it had been risky, probably rushed. Gustav had been out for the count when I left, but he could have woken up at any moment. Perhaps he had stirred in his sleep, even started to wake when the killer approached. Maybe a late night dog walker or horny teenage couple happened by just as they reached for the syringe.

The killer could have panicked, misjudged the injection so it left a mark, didn't spot the spec of blood in the dark. And if it hadn't been for whatever forced them to rush, wouldn't Gustav Lindström's death have seemed like another senseless tragedy? The odds may be low that a young, fit guy would have a sudden heart attack, but it wasn't impossible. Given his size it was hardly out the question he had at least dabbled in steroids at some point, that plus extreme exercise could have put an undue strain on his heart. If it wasn't for the careless puncture wound, it might have been impossible to tell.

Gustav and Sanna's long relationship meant that they must know dozens, hundreds of people in common. It was far from out the question that someone who knew them both harboured some sort of grudge against them both that turned rancid and into murder. But something about that didn't sit right.

Sanna's murder wasn't the first time the killer had struck, I thought. Despite the saying, getting away with murder is far from easy. Even serial killers, those white whales of criminals, rarely succeed on their first attempt. The stress of taking another life, even for the coldest of psychopaths, causes mistakes, mess, forgotten loose ends.

Sanna's murder was almost flawless. The upturned kayak appearing days later; her body lost for so long that almost all possible evidence was eradicated. The little beach where I found her was rarely used, tucked away at the back of the cottage. If it hadn't been for me storming off in a strop and getting lost, the skeleton could have lain tangled in those reeds for months, years, forever more.

It was, I thought cynically, very nearly the perfect crime.

I pulled out my phone and drummed my fingers on the screen for a second. There's little more irritating than wanting to look something up when you don't even know the words to Google. After a moment, I pulled out my notebook, made a list of the terms in English I wanted to search for, painstakingly translated each one, and started searching.

I don't know how much time passed as I sat on the bench frantically scribbling notes, but by the time I looked up again, a pale dawn was breaking overhead, and the air was filled with the scent of fresh flowers being unpacked at the stall across the square. I stretched my neck from side to side wincing as my shoulder muscles protested, and wondered if the fresh coffee I could smell brewing some-where nearby was a mirage.

Sven Olafsson, 49. Died of an asthma attack in Tantolunden Park

Annette Björkstedt, 38. Fell down the stairs opposite Fotografiska, catastrophic head injury.

Cattis Bergman, 23. Complications from an epileptic seizure at home on Skånegatan.

Sigge Åstrand, 34. Heart attack at Kvarnen.

Björne Svensson, 29. Overdose at home on Åsögatan.

Five deaths — seven, counting Sanna Johansson and Gustav Lindström — that had all occurred over the past ten years, all on this island. Except for Sanna, but she lived here. That was a lot of random tragedies in one small area. People rarely die of asthma attacks these days, or just forget to take life saving medication, I thought. Not this often.

There didn't appear to be any particular connection between the victims. Both genders, a range of ages, profes-sions, lifestyles, as far as I could see. But that was another Hollywood myth. On screen, serial killers fetishise their victims, preying on attractive brunettes to exact revenge on their mother or skinny blondes to relive their first love. In life, they're more likely to kill who they can, when they can.

It was one of the reasons they manage to get away with it for so long.

28

Y ou thought you'd got away with it. You thought no one had seen you, but I had. I saw that tiny smile of triumph flash across your face as you finally slipped to the back of the room then out the door, and it made me curious, so I followed.

That's the tragic irony of the whole thing. I only followed you because I was curious. I don't know what to say, it honestly was no more than that. If I'd been looking in the other direction when you reached the door, if I'd never noticed you moving in the first place, if something had distracted me before I got to the door, how different everything would have been.

It says so much that no one called over, shouted me to join them as I crossed the room. Unlike you, I'm rarely invisible. But that night I was. I just got up and left and no one stopped me. No one even noticed I was gone.

Doesn't that tell you it was fate?

I don't mean that to insult you, by the way. I don't mean to undermine the importance of what happened between us. In fact, if anything, the fact that it was all down to chance, to the random happenstance of you catching my eye as I yawned, makes it all *the more momentous to me. It was meant to happen. Written in the stars. Destiny. Whatever you want to call it.*

We were always going to end up in the darkness out there that night. You were always going to be the one.

You once talked about impact. We were discussing the meaning of life, debating whether achievement, making one's mark on the world, was the indication of a life truly lived. You got very defensive. You argued passionately that a life of content-ment, of family love and hobbies and small acts of kindness and so on, was just as worthy. We were all quite surprised to see the mouse roar.

But weren't your parents well-known? Politicians, something like that? I imagine that's where your defensiveness came from. Already you knew you would never live up to them. You were preparing your own defence, pretending that insignificance didn't matter. You were desperate to believe that you would still count.

Well you did count, in the end. In the end, you had more impact than you could ever have known.

You made me.

I didn't go out the same door as you. I'm not that stupid. I'd guessed, by the time I'd laced up my snow boots, where you were headed, so I took my time, knowing I could catch up easily enough.

I didn't predict you would be on skis. You must have been prepared, must have hidden them somewhere in the little yard behind the door you went out of. The skis were stored at the other end of the cabin.

You had planned your escape.

A little flame of respect flickered to life in me when I realised that. You were more interesting than I had suspected. Worthy, even.

I think that was the moment that sealed your fate.

Which is crazy when you think about it. A pair of cross

country skis, old and battered and scratched, signed your warrant. Ridiculous. It's when I remember things like that, that I wonder if I am crazy.

I mean, I am. I must be. Look at what I've done. Look at what I did to you.

That's not normal behaviour, normal impulses, I know that. I'm not in any denial over the truth of myself. I realise it must seem that way — how can I live a normal life knowing what I am, what I've done? I wonder it myself. More often than you'd think.

The morning after is the hardest. I wake up. I shower and make coffee. Get dressed, listen to the morning news, pour a second coffee into my reusable travel mug, maybe even text with a friend with one hand as I lock the door behind me. All the while, adrenaline fizzes and stings as it drains from my body, and it makes me feel detached. Uncoupled from the world somehow.

You know how, in a dream, you're never fully present? You believe in the world of the dream, you're in it for the moment, but there's a part of you held back, observing what's happening. On some level, you are conscious of the fact that you are dreaming.

That's how I feel on the mornings after. I go through the motions of life, and all the while I'm watching myself from a distance. Marvelling at how normal I seem, how no one would ever guess. Shaking my head in wonder as I give way to another cyclist, greet my colleagues, wake up my computer and yawn. Think about lunch. Decide I've had enough coffee already. I know it sounds big headed, but I'm quite astonished by myself on those mornings.

I know it's terrible, but I feel a little proud. I can't help but suspect that not everyone would be able to pull it off to the extent I do. A weaker specimen would be shaky, distracted, obviously out of sorts. It would be written all over their face. People would notice.

Of course, people never notice, do they? They never suspect.

'We had no idea. He always seemed like a lovely person. Friendly, you know. Maybe a little quiet, sometimes, now we think about it. But the nicest neighbour you could ask for. We could never have predicted what he was capable of.'

29

T he restaurant where Mia had organised a dinner to celebrate something or other was a tiny little place surrounded by a large outdoor terrace on a square in the city centre. The bar staff looked as though they had just stepped out of a Calvin Klein ad. They were shaking cocktails with more flourish than was strictly necessary, and everything was bathed in the pink glow of overhead heaters. It was the sort of swanky affair that made me want to kick off my shoes and do a can-can while belting out *My Old Man*.

If there's such a thing as being an inverted food snob, I'm it. One glance at the English version of the menu had revealed it to be all a *créme* of this and *jus* of that, so I was already grouchy and eyeing up the McDonalds across the square. My bouche does not want amusement, it wants fed. Give me a post-club bacon sarnie any day, thank you very much. Preferably from a manky little hole in the wall where the water marks on the cutlery reassure you they've been at least washed, after a fashion and no matter what time of day or night it is, you'll be served by a furious person in a filthy apron.

There was an enterprising kebab van, once upon a time, that would pull up outside — I want to say Fabric, but I can't remember for certain anymore — and dole out hundreds upon hundreds of the greasiest, most minging kebabs you could fathom. Fashionistas who normally wouldn't touch a morsel that wasn't vegan and gluten-free and had had all the toxins and calories sucked out by a Peruvian mountain goat or something queued for miles as a grimy dawn broke over London.

I was the only person I knew who never got food poisoning from it. It was my thing. I was infamous for it. *There goes Ellie. She can eat those kebabs without spending the following twelve hours curled around a toilet bowl howling for a death that's swift and merciful. It's really her. Ask for a picture if you want, she's very approachable.*

Johan had wandered off as soon as we'd arrived, of course. Things had been a touch tense between us the past few days. I hadn't told him what had happened with Gustav and the police. I know I should have, and I would, obviously, as soon as I found the right time.

It was just that, when I'd finally got home that morning, he'd been waiting, worried out of his mind. My mind was racing, grappling with the possibility of a string of murders, and it had sort of slipped my mind that I'd been out all night and hadn't let him know. He was so wound up, pacing around the tiny living area, claustrophobia rolling off him in waves as though the flat couldn't contain his worry. I thought of all the times he and his mum must have waited all night for his dad to roll in and I felt horrific. The police had offered to ring him. I should have let them.

But it was too late by then, so I told him that I'd ended

up crashing at Maddie and Lena's, and that I could have sworn I'd texted him but must have failed to properly tap Send. I fell all over myself apologising, swearing blind it would never happen again and that I felt terrible and I loved him and please, please could he forgive me. Eventually he cracked and took me in his arms I felt this massive lump in my throat as the actual truth of my night came crashing over me.

I knew that if I let the tiniest tear escape I'd fall apart, so I pulled back and pretended I needed the loo. When I came out he'd made me breakfast. He kissed the top of my head and dashed out for work, looking exhausted and drained. I tucked into the most gorgeous pancakes, feeling like the worst person ever to walk the earth.

I'd been wound up like a spring ever since. Every time I heard someone in the hallway outside his flat I'd tensed, bracing myself for the police to bang on the door. A siren had zipped up the road the night before and I'd jumped a mile in bed, sitting up bolt outright and waking Johan. He assumed I'd had a nightmare and was so sweet trying to comfort me it nearly made me cry again.

It would be fine, I reminded myself, again. If the police wanted to talk to me, then I would explain everything to Johan. Maybe I'd be able to skirt round the fact it would be the second interview. Maybe not. Either way, if they didn't, there was no need to worry him.

In the meantime, I was pleased he was getting a chance to relax and hang out with his friends, and I could take care of myself. Deciding to take Maddie's lead and just bulldoze my way into conversations, I introduced myself to a group of guys hanging by the bar. They all politely shook my hand, then continued to chat in Swedish while I stood there with an inane grin pasted on my face. *Strike one.*

I then turned to some random woman and complimented her on her dress, even though, truth be told, it was a plain black shift so what really was there to say about it? She smiled and thanked me, then turned to greet someone else and I more or less got a mouthful of her hair. *Strike two.*

I know the traditional approach is three strikes, but at that point I didn't have the heart and I didn't want to stand there on my own like a wally, so I went to the loo and hid for a bit.

When I decided to brave the masses again, everyone had taken their seats for dinner. And there were no seats left near Johan. He was deep in conversation with some guy as I approached the table, all settled in with his napkin on his lap and his wine glass already filled. He didn't even look up. Liv was next to him — *of course* — and Krister was opposite, laughing at something Liv had said.

I couldn't see Mia. She'd be busy, flittering about playing hostess and making sure everything was going to plan. It crossed my mind to find her and pointedly ask her where I should sit, then realised it would be a bit like going to the teacher to complain no one would play with me. I pictured Mia leading me back to the table by the hand, sternly telling everyone to be nice to Ellie or she would have a word with their mums.

The table was long and narrow, with thirty odd people seated along it, which did little to dislodge the feeling that it was all a bit school dinners. I made my way down to the far end, firmly telling myself I was imagining that it was only more dimly lit down in the hinterlands. I couldn't be exiled from the cool kids' section because we were adults and there was no such thing.

As I took my seat, a freckly woman with a sunburned nose flashed me a bright grin and held out her hand.

'*Hej! Jag heter Corinna. Vem är du?*'

Well this was a turn up for the books. She looked at me expectantly. *Heter,* I thought frantically. Name. She's asking my name, or telling me hers. Eventually I gave up with an apologetic grin.

'I'm so sorry, I don't speak Swedish. I'm Ellie.'

'Oh you're British, how exciting. I am Corinna, and this is Magnus, Kalle and Sven.'

The three guys to the left of us were the same I'd introduced myself to at the bar. They all nodded briefly in my direction, clearly having zero recollection of me from not fifteen minutes earlier.

It turned out that Corinna had lived in New York for a few years in her early twenties. 'The first few guys I dated, they couldn't stop talking about how amazing I was, how they had been looking forward to the date all day, how excited they were to get to know me, so of course I was terrified they were all in love with me,' she grinned as she refilled my wine glass.

'Just before I left Sweden, one of my friends got engaged, and at the party to celebrate she drunkenly confessed that until he proposed she had no idea whether or not he was in to her. To me that's normal,' she added. 'So these American guys who were so full of compliments — I was like *shit, I'm going to have to start breaking some hearts here.* And then none of them called.'

I laughed. 'I think English guys are a bit more like Swedish that way, at least.'

'So what made you move to Sweden? Was it for a man?'

I don't know what made me hesitate. Maybe it was the sound of Liv's voice. Maybe it was the little glimpses I kept getting of Johan laughing with his friends, a million miles away from me.

'I'm a journalist,' I said finally. It wasn't a lie. 'I'm — I'm actually working on a story, about a possible serial killer operating in Stockholm.' It wasn't entirely a lie.

Corinna's eyes widened and she leaned in. 'Really? How thrilling. And dangerous, or?'

I shrugged. 'Not unless they know I'm on to them.'

'You said possible serial killer — are you not certain?'

'I'm certain,' I said, realising at that moment that it was true. 'But I can't prove it yet.'

'And do the police know?'

'I don't think so, not yet.'

'It's just so interesting. I'm sorry, do you think I'm strange? It's just that I love true crime, you know, all those podcasts and things. I am a historian, and a lot of my job involves figuring out puzzles. What is this person referring to in that letter and what does it tell us about what else they say? Maybe that is why I like puzzles for fun, also.'

'Wow, that is so cool.'

'It is,' she smiled. 'I love my job.'

'What period do you specialise in?'

'Quite recent really, the Cold War. I am fascinated by how much we are affected by wars we claim we are not part of.' Silent waiters refilled both of our wine glasses. Corinna nodded her thanks and took a sip of hers. Out of the corner of my eye, I could see Johan and Liv laughing, but I firmly kept my focus on Corinna. 'In my thesis,' she continued, her eyes sparking with passion, 'I argue that Sweden could not truly be considered neutral because of how much we cooperated with the Americans. '

'I've heard something about that — have you talked to Krister about his family's summer cottage? He was telling me how the Americans might have used it for a base.'

She nodded. 'Yes of course. I found some documents

relating to their bunker, in fact.'

'Wow, he'll be thrilled to hear that.'

A frown flickered across Corinna's face and I guessed that Krister hadn't been as appreciative of her hard work as he might have been. I could just picture his patronising little smirk. I heard Liv shout, a joking protest, and I glanced over to see her mock shoving Johan as he raised his hands in surrender.

'Do you know them?' asked Corinna, following my gaze.

'Not really,' I said.

Just then a cheer went up as Mia stood up to make a little speech that I wouldn't have understood even if I could hear it properly from the other end of the table. Magnus or Kalle or Sven handed me a shot and a chorus of *skåls* rang around the table. I raised my glass and downed my shot, grimacing as it just about melted my throat.

'Anyway, it is so fascinating to meet a real life investigator, I feel quite starstruck,' Corinna smiled. 'I don't know what makes me so interested in true crime, but I do love it.'

I smiled. 'I think for a lot of people it's because it could happen to any of us. Not just being the victim either. I once interviewed a Detective Chief Inspector of the Met Police in London, and I asked him if anyone could potentially become a murderer, or was it something you were either born with or not. He said yes, pretty much anyone was theoretically capable given the right circumstances.'

'I agree with that,' Corinna nodded. 'I think I could.' She smiled. 'I hope I don't ever have to, but if I was threatened, or my family, my nieces or nephews maybe? I don't even think I would find it so hard. Perhaps that is the true fascination,' she added, thinking it over. 'We all imagine we are so cosy and safe and protected, with the police and army to keep that sort of pain and tragedy far away from us. We think we are so far away from the darkest parts of human nature, that things like murder only happen in Hollywood films.'

I nodded. 'Exactly. But it's closer than we think.'

'There was a woman I used to work with who believed her husband was murdered,' Corinna said. She lowered her voice, leaned in a bit more. 'Everyone said she was crazy, that it was just grief talking. But sometimes I wonder.'

'How did he die?' I asked.

'He took an overdose,' she said. 'If I remember correctly, he had some sort of chronic pain condition. Something to do with his spine, I think, but it was under control. He did a lot of yoga, which also helped, and I met him at classes two or three times. I liked him a lot. He was warm, easy to talk to. And they seemed a really great couple. Sometimes — I don't know if you're single, but sometimes for me the hardest thing is that I don't envy so many of my friends' relationships. I want to,' she added with a wry grin. 'I wish I could say *I want that,* but so much of the time I am thinking more — shit, what is the English phrase?'

'Rather you than me?' I supplied.

'Yes! Exactly.' She laughed and made a face. 'But Björne and Tove, they were one couple I envied. There was something about them that was just —' She shrugged. 'They fit. He was quiet, while she could be wild and funny, but they were so comfortable together.

'Anyway, one Saturday morning she went out for a run. He was still asleep when she left, and when she got back he was slumped on their kitchen table, an empty bottle of his pain medication in his hand.'

'That's awful.'

'It was terrible. I hardly knew them, but I felt almost as though I grieved too. It was such a tragedy. And Tove —'

Corina shook her head. 'She has never been the same. It was more than grief. She is convinced that he did not do it, and became obsessed by proving it was murder. Most people believe that she just cannot bring herself to accept that he would leave her, but sometimes I am not so sure. Nobody knew him better than she did. Sometimes I feel that people dismiss her because the thought of murder is just so huge, so horrifying, that it's like crossing a line to even consider the possibility.'

'Does she have any reason beyond her gut feeling to suspect someone else was involved?' I asked. My mind was racing. Björne. Björne Svensson? *Overdose on Åsögatan.*

'She claims she is certain she locked the door behind her when she left, because he was still asleep, and that when she got back it was open. She said that they normally didn't bother to lock the door when they are home, but why would he have unlocked it? It could only be that he opened the door to let someone in.'

'She told the police all this, I take it?'

Corinna nodded. 'Many times. She once said to me that she knew they thought she was nuts but she didn't care any more. She hoped that, at least, they might do something about it, even if just to get her to stop bothering them. I believe she finally persuaded them to test the pill bottle for fingerprints, but they found only his.'

'Are you still in touch with her?'

'I haven't spoken to her in a while. She left her job maybe six months ago, and I keep meaning to call or text.' Corinna shrugged, with a guilty smile. 'You know what it's like. I will call her tomorrow though.'

'If you do, do you think you could ask her if she would speak to me?' I asked.

'Of course.'

30

T here was no Svensson listed on the buzzer outside the building where Björne and Tove Svensson lived on Åsögatan. I hadn't heard from Corinna, but a bit of Googling had revealed their address, so I decided to take a chance with some good old fashioned doorstepping. Surely if Tove was determined to prove her husband's death was murder, she would be happy to speak to me.

I didn't know the code for the door, but there was a fancy restaurant just next door, so I hung about pretending to read the menu for a while. Finally, a young dad with a toddler on his shoulders came out, and I grabbed the door before it shut behind him.

There was a lovely smell in the lobby, some kind of polishing oil, I guessed. Next to the little concertina-doored lift was a gleaming brass plaque listing all the residents. *Svensson — 3tr.*

Bingo, I thought, taking the stairs two at a time to reach the third floor.

There were two flats on each little landing, but all the way up the stairs I couldn't hear a peep from anyone inside.

It was eerily silent, as though the building itself was asleep. Although I was still in a communal area, I already felt as though I were intruding and I hesitated in front of Tove Svensson's front door, trying to decide whether disturbing her would be a mistake. Maybe I should wait until Corinna had sounded her out first. I was just toying with trying to message Corinna again when the door across the landing opened and I jumped a mile.

A middle aged guy emerged, handsome in a weather-beaten sort of way. He looked exhausted, deep crevices around his eyes and he barely glanced in my direction, as though his mouth didn't have the energy to smile. He carried a laundry basket, and from somewhere inside his flat I could hear a baby wail as he shut the door behind him.

'I just realised how early it is,' I blurted. He looked at me, startled. I nodded towards Tove Svensson's front door. 'I don't want to disturb her.'

'They are on vacation,' he said, a bit haltingly, as though his English was rarely used.

'They?' I frowned. She couldn't have met someone else, surely? That didn't sound likely, from what Corinna had said about her. Maybe she had a flatmate.

'Visiting her family, I think. In Estonia.' The guy's expression hardened, suddenly, as though it had just occurred to him to be suspicious. 'Are you a friend?'

'I — perhaps I got the wrong flat. I'm looking for Tove Svensson?'

He shook his head. 'It is Hampus and Kaisa Svensson who live there.' He smiled briefly. 'Svensson is quite a common name.'

'Shit, there must have been two listed and I didn't realise. Sorry. Thanks for letting me know.'

I turned to head down the stairs, then something in his expression caught my eye.

'Tove Svensson?' he said. 'Who was married to Björne Svensson?'

I nodded.

'They did live here, over in the gårdhus.'

'Did? Did she move?' I said, my heart sinking. 'This was the only address for her I could find.'

'What do you want with her?' he asked, a steely edge to his voice.

I hesitated. 'I want to talk to her about her husband's death,' I said. 'I don't want to bother her, I want to help.'

'Well you are too late,' he said. 'Tove Svensson is dead.'

31

---

*T*ove Svensson was dead because she wouldn't stop asking questions about her husband, I thought. It was a gorgeous late summer day, the sky a startling blue, sun glinting off the brightly coloured apartment buildings all around me. There was a display of flower bouquets outside the 7-Eleven on the corner and a group of friends laughed as they headed in to the yoga studio across the road.

I made my way to the little coffee shop I loved, where Liv had blanked me all those weeks ago. It was rammed with Sunday morning brunchers, clamouring for tables in the sunshine, but I managed to nab the last tiny one. As I stared blindly at the fountain glistening in the sun in the little park where Gustav Lindström died, I could feel a tremor, deep within me. Forcing myself to steady my breathing, I took out my phone and toyed with it a moment, trying to work up the courage to start searching.

A group of kids screamed as they splashed in the fountain.

A baby cried at the table next to me.

People screamed and laughed as the wind changed, splattering the fountain over some picnickers.

Finally I forced myself to open my phone.

Car crash.

I understood the photo of the wrecked car, half submerged in a ditch, surrounded by crime scene tape, guarded by a grim faced police officer, even before the translation app did its magic. Tove Svensson died when her car plunged off an icy verge on the E4 motorway just beyond Sollentuna. She had taken two sleeping pills and dozed off at the wheel.

My heart started to pound. A guy approached, gestured to the second chair at my table, presumably asked if he could take it. I jumped and stared at him with such horror that he backed away with an apologetic smile, holding up his hands in surrender.

The packet of sleeping pills was found in Tove's handbag under the passenger seat. It was a simple, over-the-counter sleep aid, the kind loads of people take the night before a big presentation, or to manage jet lag. A packet of the same brand's painkiller was also found in the bag, and the verdict suggested she had confused the two and taken the sleeping pill before driving by mistake.

Except she hadn't, I thought, little tingles of horror breaking out over me. Another tragic accident to add to the list. I looked around the square. There were young couples snuggling together on the grass. Families heading for the swings. People reading alone in the sunshine on the cobblestoned lane, cycling past waving to friends, moseying at the rack of vintage clothes outside the second hand shop.

Any one of them could meet a *tragic accident* at any moment.

I opened up my phone again and messaged Corinna. I didn't want to break the news of her friend's death in a text, so I just asked her to get in touch with me urgently. When I checked the message a few minutes later, I saw it had been read, but she never answered.

32

'I don't know babe, it sounds a bit — I mean, fuck, a serial killer?' Maddie glanced over at Lena, her eyes worried. Lena's expression remained impassive as she thought it over. We were sitting on their teensy balcony, the sun beating down. In the yard below someone was barbequing, the smell reminding me I'd clean forgotten breakfast and lunch.

'Well what are the chances?' I said. 'Sanna took pills and died, Björne took pills and died, Tove took pills and died. I don't believe in that many coincidences.'

'Tove took pills and died after almost two years of being out of her mind with grief,' Maddie said gently. 'It might not be a coincidence, but that doesn't make it murder.'

'What about Gustav?' I persisted. 'He was injected with something. Someone must have done that for a reason.'

'For all we know, he was dealing steroids, or had who-knows-what going on in his life,' Maddie said gently. 'We told the police what time you got here that night and I got the impression it ruled you out, but they won't thank you for sticking your nose in. I'm worried it won't look good for you, whether you're on to something or not.'

'I think I agree with Ellie,' Lena spoke up finally. 'Accidents and tragedies do happen, but I agree that for so many people in such a small area to have been careless with medication —' She shrugged. 'It is worrying. But Maddie is right that you must be very careful.'

'Well thanks judge and jury,' Maddie grinned, leaning over to kiss Lena. 'Glad I'm right about some things.'

'But you do think it's possible someone has been doing this?'

'Yes,' Lena said simply. 'At least, I think it must be investigated.'

'The thought of somebody quietly killing for years like this is chilling,' Maddie said. 'Like, they're not doing it for revenge or to make some kind of sick point, but just to kill— it's so cold. I read somewhere that serial killers get off on all the fear and pandemonium they cause. It's often the killer himself who calls in tips to media, just to enjoy the uproar. They even get involved in the investigation sometimes, pretending to be a witness, playing this high stakes game with the police. But this person doesn't need any of that. They're just killing for their own private satisfaction.'

'They weren't controlled about Gustav,' I pointed out. 'That was the first time they've left behind any hint another person was involved at all.'

'That's what frightens me babe. If they're starting to lose control —' Maddie cut herself off, squeezed my hand.

'I spoke to a friend who works in the lab about the case,' Lena said. 'The tox screening on Gustav Lindström's body came back completely clean.'

'What? How could it be clean when he was injected?' Maddie asked.

Lena shrugged. 'He must have been injected with something that was undetectable just a few hours later.'

156 CS DUFFY

'How is that possible?'

'I don't know enough about chemistry to say, I just know there are some drugs that do not show up, at least not on the standard tests.'

'So if it wasn't for the puncture wound and the blood on his collar, it would have looked like a natural heart attack,' I said. 'Albeit an unlikely one.'

Lena nodded.

'There was another heart attack on the list of possible victims I made. Another young guy, thirty-four I think. He was dancing at some club and started to fit. People around him thought he was having a bad reaction to alcohol or drugs, but he was found to have been almost sober, no drugs in his system.' I pulled out my phone and opened the notebook where I'd saved all the links, found the one I wanted and passed it to Lena.

'The drug acted very fast on Gustav Lindström, there was only minutes between you leaving and his death,' she muttered, skimming the article. 'So this guy, Sigge Åstrand, must have been injected when he was already at Kvarnen.'

I'd been to Kvarnen once, with Johan, for dinner. It was like an old fashioned beer tavern upstairs, and a sweaty club downstairs. 'If you are, like, twenty-two and you haven't found someone to go home with by midnight on a Friday,' Johan had grinned when he caught me watching the teenagers streaming downstairs, 'you head down there and take what's left. It is a wonderful system. Everybody is happy.'

'Could it have happened in the gents'?' I said.

'A guy bashing into another guy in the men's room would get his head kicked in pretty quick-smart where I come from,' Maddie said sourly. 'Maybe some Swedes are more evolved, but it would be pretty risky if you ask me.'

'If this drug works that fast he might not have had time to react. Or maybe it happened on the dance floor. If it was crowded then it's possible that no one would have seen the injection.'

'Still risky, I reckon.' Maddie shook her head.

'I don't disagree,' I said, 'but this person has been literally getting away with murder for years. He knows what he's doing and he's as confident as fuck.'

'Wouldn't they have CCTV at this bar?' asked Maddie.

'They probably have some system,' Lena said, 'it might have even been checked at the time, but it is two years later. Any footage will be long gone.'

I sighed in frustration. 'This bastard is too good at this,' I said. 'Maddie's right. It's chilling. Generally, there's a bit of a connection between lack of control, lack of problem solving skills and criminality, right? That's why the vast majority get caught sooner or later. The famous unsolved cases, like Jack the Ripper or whoever, they're legendary because it's not normal to escape justice. But if all these people have been murdered by the same person, then this killer has been at large for years and years. They're a bloody maestro at it.'

'When was the earliest of these accidental deaths you could find?' asked Lena.

'2007,' I said. 'More than a decade ago. And there might well be more, my search probably wasn't exhaustive.'

'There is one more you should perhaps look at,' Lena said, squinting against the sinking sun as she thought. 'I went to high school on Söder. My father lived at Hornstull. When we were in the final year, there was a ski trip, and someone died. Karin Söderström. She had epilepsy. We all knew it, a nurse had come in to school to teach us all what to do if she had a fit. But during the trip, she snuck out of the cabin one evening, and went skiing. She never told anyone she was going. She was very quiet, wasn't unliked but also wasn't exactly a part of the group, you know?

'Earlier that day, some of us had been discussing going for a moonlight ski, but when it came to evening and it was warm around the fire, the idea did not seem like so much fun any more. But I guess Karin still thought it was, because she went out. The following day she was found on one of the trails behind the cabin. She had had an attack and fell unconscious, then the cold killed her. She was sixteen.'

'That's awful,' Maddie said quietly, rubbing Lena's arm.

'I wasn't close friends with her, but we both worked in the school library, and we talked a few times. She was a nice girl. Shy, but very sweet.' Lena fell silent a moment. Maddie and I waited. 'I never believed that Karin would go out at night without her medicine,' she said finally. 'She was so careful. She told me once it can be possible to feel an attack coming, and that if she began to feel a fuzzy or tingly feeling approaching she knew she had moments to get to her medicine in time. She practiced over and over, like a military drill. When she was found that morning on the path, she did not have any medication with her. At the time I just thought maybe I did not know her as well as I thought. Now I am not so sure.'

'If the same person got her, they have been killing for what, fifteen years?' Maddie said in horror.

'And they must be connected to your school,' I said. 'A teacher?'

Lena got up and grabbed an old photograph album from a box on the bookshelf. 'This album is from the year of that trip,' she said, leafing through the pages. I looked over her shoulder, smiling at how everyone's school photos look alike. These might feature taller and blonder people, but they were still the same gawky teenagers with shocking fashion choices as in my albums. 'I think there are some photos from the trip —'

'That's Mia,' I blurted, tapping the photo of a much younger Mia making a face at the camera.

'Do you know Mia?' said Lena in surprise. 'She organised a fundraiser party in Karin's memory. She was one of the cool kids, but she was the nicest one as I recall.'

'Yeah, I know her,' I muttered, turning the page. 'And there she is with Krister. Can I borrow that one? They could use it for a wedding invitation or something.'

'Mia and Krister are getting married?' said Lena in surprise. 'I never would have predicted they would be in touch even, how funny.'

'Yeah. I don't really know him all that well, but she is lovely.'

'And what about Johan and Liv? Do you know them? Are they still together?'

33

T he busses were off because of the snow so I had walked home. I quite enjoy walking through crazy weather like that, when it is so cold you feel your breath icy in your lungs, and snow coats your nose and mouth. I wasn't frustrated or enraged or consumed with self loathing. I felt really quite content. Happy, even.

I was hungry, I remember that. I stopped at the hot dog stand on Södermalmstorg, and ate the hot, spicy treat walking up Katrinavägen. The air was thick and heavy with snow, the sky glowing the greyish pink of deepest winter. I could only just make out the shadowy hulks of ships in the harbour, and the city centre was invisible altogether, melted into the murk in the distance.

I'd passed a handful of people along the way, but everyone was so wrapped up, scarves wound over noses, heads bent, braced against the worst of the icy wind, hands deep in pockets of enormous quilted coats. They barely looked human. With the thick snow muffling the sounds of the city, it was almost like being alone.

I'm not sure what made you catch my eye. At the time, I still *had no idea what made me chose, I didn't even wonder. I noticed you, and that was all that mattered.*

We were at the top of the hill. You'd stopped in front of the vegetarian restaurant, and were reading the menu with a frown, even though I'm almost certain it closes in winter. It crossed my mind to tell you that, then I decided I didn't care. I stood by the top of the staircase cut into the cliff that leads to Fotografiska below, my hands in my pockets, though I couldn't feel the cold any more. Something was warming me from within. I must have already decided.

A huge cruise liner was gliding into the harbour, so gigantic that the top of it was level with my eye line, even though I stood on a cliff high above. It must have been around 6pm in that case, as that is the time the ships arrive from the Baltic States. That made sense, I had left work a little after five.

I watched it emerge with eerie silence from the shadowy fog, but my every cell, every atom was focussed on you. That's the bit no one will ever understand. How amazing I feel. How dominant. The way my entire being zings with power, with awareness, with the very universe flooding through me.

The vikings used to believe that if they killed a warrior in battle they would consume his life force, and that enough kills, enough life forces attained, would make them immortal. Of course I don't believe I am immortal, I'm not a child. But I know the force that floods through me with each kill. How I crave it with a ravenous urge that makes my blood itch. How I never feel more truly alive than when I take a life.

It frustrates me that I can never remember the moment it happens. One minute the certainty of what is about to happen illuminates me from within, and then it is over and everything goes dark. It's as though when I switch the light off in you, some-thing inside me dies too.

So you see, it's not as though it isn't hard on me.

Generally, I don't even allow myself the thrill of watching the light in your eyes switch off. Once I did. Not you, I could barely make out your broken body in the darkness from so far above — though I did in your case get to hear screams and sirens. I think a car might have crashed into the central reservation, presumably trying to avoid you, though what on earth was the point after the fall you'd had? A few tire tracks would hardly have made a difference, the chaos was entirely unnecessary. Stadsgårdsleden was closed for hours, on a weekday evening, at the height of rush hour. Normally whatever happens next doesn't particularly interest me, but I have to admit I had a giggle at that.

It was one of the others, I can't even remember who now.

Yes I do — the little man with the glasses in Tantolunden Park. He was begging me to help him, to call an ambulance, to help him find his inhaler. Then he just stopped. He went quiet and simply stared at me, as it must have dawned on him that I was not there to help. That was interesting to watch. His eyes went dark and desperate, then nothing. Just, blank.

Dead, after all.

Perhaps I'm being obvious. I hate to be obvious. It was quite disappointing, to tell the truth. I never took the risk of hanging around again. It wasn't worth it.

There was one I would have quite liked to have watched, of course. It would have been satisfying to see her struggle. To hear the gasping, choking, gurgling breaths as water filled her lungs and dragged her inexorably below. She wouldn't have begged, though. She wouldn't have given me the satisfaction. Besides, she would already have known I was never going to help her.

It's not as though I hadn't known, deep down, all along. Of course I had. Ever since I saw them at the Midsummer table as I slipped into the woods. The intimacy between them had been unmistakeable.

I just chose to mistake it.

Something must have happened to break them up, but it wasn't over between them. We were just distractions, Sanna and I. No wonder Liv could barely bring herself to look at us.

Well, good to know. I'd book a flight in the morning. That was that, then. Sorted.

I tried to push aside the heavy, leaden pain, as I walked down the hill towards Johan's old high school. Everywhere I looked I could see a teenaged Johan and Liv. Dawdling hand-in-hand outside the playing fields, snogging in front of the little corner shop, sitting on that wall overlooking the old railway tracks, dangling their feet as they made plans for their lives together.

Don't get me wrong, it wasn't the fact they had been a

couple. I hardly imagined Johan had been a virgin when we met, for Heaven's sake. Of course he'd had a past.

Or at least, it wasn't just that they had been a couple.

But he had lied. There were no two ways about that. I'd asked him about the history of his friends and he had chosen not to include the fact that he and Liv had once been in love. It had hardly slipped his mind. It was lying by omission. He had deliberately left me out in the cold.

Hot tears prickled at my eye as I thought of her barging into his flat and pouring her heart out to him on the couch that night. *Boy trouble*, he'd told me. Too right she had boy trouble. The man she loved had moved some random from London into his flat. The idea of them discussing their relationship, talking about me, all the while I'd been right there and didn't have a clue, made me want to scream.

Won't that be a bit rubbish for her, spending the weekend with two couples? I'd asked Johan as we waited for Krister on the jetty at Midsummer. I'd been lying too.

I'd been pretending to be sympathetic about poor, single Liv, when really I'd been smug, thinking I was on the inside for once. But it had been me on the outside. It had been me spending the weekend with two couples. I should have bloody known.

The lump in my throat ached and I could feel a sob building as I reached the gates of the school. I couldn't do this now, I thought with rising panic. I didn't have time. I'd have to pencil a little cry into my diary for some other time.

'Ellie?'

At the front door of the school, principal Josefin Beckmann held out her hand with a friendly smile. She must have been sixty at least, though her hair was blonde, piled in a thick ballet bun on top of her head. She was deeply tanned, the crinkles around her eyes suggesting a lifetime of laughter.

'Thank you so much for meeting me,' I said, shaking her hand.

She nodded and gestured for me to follow her along a long corridor bordered with lockers. That school smell of polish, school dinners and trainers pervaded the air, though the halls were deserted and our footsteps echoed.

'There are some summer programs running,' Josefin said as she opened the door of a cosy little office. 'But today, everyone is outside enjoying the sunshine. I always think empty schools are a little spooky. What is a school without children?'

I took a seat on the little sofa she gestured to, stuffed against the back wall of her office beneath shelves heaving with box files and books. There were framed certificates and newspaper articles covering the wall next to me. I couldn't read the headlines, but a quick glance at the photos suggested the clippings were celebrating former student triumphs. There was a cosy warmth to the room, with slightly tatty furniture and the prominent wall of pride. I could imagine finding sanctuary here as a teenager, I thought, pouring my heart out to Josefin Beckmann about exam worries or troubles at home. She was the sort of person who made everything better.

'I appreciate your being willing to talk to me,' I said.

'It was many years ago, but I will do my best to help.'

'As I explained over email, I am looking in to a series of accidental or otherwise natural deaths that have happened in this area over the past fifteen years or so.'

'You don't think they are accidents?'

'I'm not certain yet. That's what I'm trying to find out.'

She nodded and sat back in her chair, her fingertips pressed together as she thought.

'How did the case of Karin Söderström come to your attention?' she asked. 'There was very little media about it. Because of her age, we were able to contain the story quite well. Her parents —' She gave a sad sigh. 'It was very difficult for them to take. She was an only child, absolutely adored, though remarkably unspoilt. I see her mother around from time to time. She still looks haunted.'

'I discussed my story with a former student of yours, who is now a police officer. She remembered what happened to Karin and wondered if there could be a connection.'

Josefin nodded, then went quiet for a long moment, her expression troubled. 'Karin was an extremely careful girl,' she said. 'She kept her medication in a little container that she wore around her neck. She once demonstrated to me how she had trained herself to automatically reach for the chain when she felt an attack coming on. She also kept an extra packet in a pocket or her backpack as back up.'

'But when she was found she didn't have any medication on her?'

Josefin shook her head. 'The principal at the time, my boss, insisted she must have forgotten in the excitement of sneaking out. She had left some skis next to the back door in preparation, you see. It wasn't an impulsive late night walk, she must have planned it. There was speculation that she intended to meet a boy.'

'I was given the impression she was on the quiet side?'

'She was. A very thoughtful, sensible girl.' Josefin smiled sadly. 'She told me once she found teenagers boring, that she couldn't wait to be old enough to have friends who thought as she did, who would also enjoy talking about books and going to museums and classical concerts. I couldn't stop thinking about that at her funeral. How she would forever be a teenager when it made her so unhappy.'

'Presumably none of the boys admitted planning to meet her that night?'

'No.' Josefin shrugged, drummed her fingernails on the arm of the chair. 'Some were questioned, but an investigation wasn't really pursued. My feeling —' She cut herself off, then sighed impatiently. 'I will be honest with you. My feeling was that the verdict of 'tragic accident' was a little convenient for the school board. Of course no school wants to invite the examination and speculation of a scandal like that, we have the other children to think of.

'But all the same, I do not believe that the matter was investigated thoroughly enough before it was closed. We questioned the students the following morning of course, and most said that they had all been in the common room watching TV all night, that no one had particularly noticed Karin or anyone else leaving. But we teachers were in a smaller room just across the hall, and I recall people walking back and forth along the corridors all evening. Most were slipping away to smoke or find beer, some to be alone with a favourite friend, perhaps. Typical things. We teachers just left them to their fun. But any one of them could have left that room to follow Karin.'

'You seem certain it was another student?'

'None of the teachers were absent for long enough. We got into quite a lively discussion about politics and sat up for much of the night, the entire group. No one left for any significant period. There were other staff in the cabin, but if you say this is a local matter then it must be either a student or teacher, which leaves a student.'

'A sixteen year old, though? It seems incredible that

someone so young could be capable of cold blooded murder.'

Josefin shrugged. 'In my experience, if there is darkness in a person, it is already present in childhood. I have encountered a few students over the years that I felt afraid to send out in to the world. According to what the police told us, it was the cold that killed Karin Söderström in the end. An epileptic attack knocked her unconscious. The killer — if there was one — may have done nothing but keep her medication from her then leave her to die.'

'What about footprints?'

'It snowed heavily all night, so any prints were long gone by morning. We almost didn't find her at all, she was buried so deeply, but luckily she had been wearing red mittens and one hand stuck just far enough out the snow to be visible. Her mother had knitted the mittens, and earlier that day I tried to persuade her to borrow some waterproof ski gloves. They were cream. If she had agreed, she might never have been found until spring.' The older woman's eyes filled up and she went quiet a moment, taking several shaky breaths.

'Was there anyone Karin didn't get on with, who might have followed her that night?' I asked gently.

'I don't believe so. As I already said, Karin was a quiet girl, kept to herself mostly. The school held a memorial assembly, to allow students to share memories of her and grieve together, and the only things they could think of to say broke my heart. *She lent me a pencil once. She gave up her seat on the bus so I could sit with my friend. She let me copy her biology homework.* Some children are like that, of course, are barely a shadow in their school years, who then blossom into a content adult. I have no doubt Karin Söderström would have done so, but she never got the chance.'

'Would you still have a list of the students who were on

that trip?'

Josefin nodded. 'I prepared one when I got your email.'

She handed me a sheet of neatly typed names from her desk. Icy chills danced over me as I read Johan, Liv, Mia, Krister. Of course they were all there.

'Have you come across any of these people in your research?' Josefin asked, searching my face. She hadn't missed my reaction. 'They would be in their early thirties or so now.'

'I would have to check my notes, but one or two are familiar,' I said, forcing a smile.

I looked up at the wall of framed clippings. 'You take a lot of pride in your former students.'

'I do, though this wall is also for inspiration. Many students now come and sit on that sofa where you are, feeling overwhelmed and anxious and afraid that they have already failed in life. I like to tell them stories of students who felt just as they did, then point to what they have achieved since.' She got up and pointed to one of the larger clippings with a fond smile. I followed her gaze, and my heart flipped over.

'Krister Larsson struggled desperately through his school years. He was very intelligent but failed several classes many times, and was almost expelled for fighting. But in the final year he knuckled down and ended up gaining one of the highest honours that Karolinska Institute awards for chemistry.'

'Chemistry?' I blurted.

Krister's face filled my mind. Those cold, dark eyes staring at me without expression.

'I believe he is now working on a drug that could cure heart disease,' Josefin said. 'If he succeeds, he may win a Nobel Prize.'

35

Mia said that she and Krister were together when Sanna disappeared, but he could have given her the pills earlier. Thoughts pierced my mind like daggers as I marched towards Götgatan. It was filled with pedestrians strolling on the cobblestones in the sunshine, a few bikes dinging warning bells as they weaved their wobbly way through the crowd.

Or she could be protecting him. He could have drugged her too. Maybe she fell asleep on that beach on the other island, and only assumed he had been by her side the whole time.

On autopilot, I made my way into a sunny coffee shop, all sleek and modern and bordered with glass walls. I must have ordered, because a moment later I was holding a steaming cup of coffee. I grabbed a table by one of the windows and stared blindly at the bustle outside as I thought.

Krister was on the ski trip. He was on the island when Sanna died. He was near the little park where Gustav Lindström died. He and Mia lived just a block or two from where

I had left her on the corner. She would have been home by the time Gustav shoved me onto the grass.

But what could she have told him that made him come out after us? Gustav had been at the same bar as us, but it was massive. I hadn't seen him there, had Mia? And even if she had, why would she have bothered to mention it to Krister?

Me.

Spiders of horror scuttled over me as I realised she would have told him she'd run into me. She might well have reported our conversation as she got ready for bed. Chatting away as she brushed her teeth, put on night cream. *She was quite curious about the day Sanna died. I suppose that's natural, isn't it? Hopefully I put her mind to rest a bit.*

She would have yawned, kissed him, snuggled down to sleep.

And he stole out into the darkness to find me.

Access and opportunity. Krister had both for Karin, Sanna and Gustav. But would that be enough for the police? What about the other victims?

Corinna, I thought. She knew Björne and Tove Svensson, and she had been at a dinner that included Krister. They too had lived within a hundred metres or so of Krister, but so did hundreds of other people. Corinna might know of a closer connection.

I pulled out my phone and opened Facebook messages to find my last message to her. She hadn't replied, but of course she had no idea what I needed to tell her. Maybe I could try to phone —

She was gone.

My heart started to thud as I stared at my phone. It couldn't be. I'd made a mistake.

There was no profile picture next to our message thread,

and her name was faded out so I couldn't click on her profile. Had she deleted her account or blocked me? My hands felt weak suddenly, and I put my phone down quickly before I dropped it.

Why would she block me? She barely knew me, had been more than friendly the only time we met. I'd only asked if we could speak in my message to her. I hadn't even hinted at what I had to tell her about Tove. Why had she cut me off?

I scanned the crowds outside, my heart hammering as it dawned on me how exposed I was. This coffee shop was nothing more than a giant fishbowl. Anyone could be watching me. Keeping tabs on what I was doing. Making sure I wasn't getting too close.

I wasn't too close, I thought in frustration. Unless I could link Krister to one of the other deaths, I had nothing. I'd already tried to find Björne Svensson's social media profiles, but there turned out to be about fourteen bajillion people named Björne Svensson in Sweden, so I'd given up.

Maybe searching Krister or Mia's friend lists would turn up something, would turn up something, some indication of how Björne Svensson, or any of the others, had made it on to Krister's radar. I opened up the list of the other victims in another window so I could cross reference.

Find the connection. Hand it to the police. Get on the next flight to London.

My to do list rattled incessantly around my head as I scrolled through Krister's profile. He rarely posted. I knew from monitoring Mia and Liv's posts that he liked them often enough to suggest he logged in regularly, but most of the activity on his wall was him being tagged in other people's posts. He had been the first of Johan's friends to send me a request, I thought wryly, remembering how thrilled I'd been. It was only a few weeks after Thailand, and I'd ran around my flat whooping for joy because Johan had told his best friend about me.

Krister Larsson is drinking beer at Kvarnen.

HEJA BAJEN!

In one of the comments below the post, Mia had uploaded a photo of Krister and Johan. Krister held a beer and was laughing at Johan, who was frozen mid roar, arms aloft, face contorted, like a Viking preparing for battle. There was no sign of Liv, but I had no doubt she was there, just out of shot, laughing adoringly at Johan.

It was the date Sigge Åstrand collapsed in the club downstairs.

I frowned. There was that feeling again, the same maddening sensation I'd had that night on Medborgarplatsen. There was a thought dancing just out of reach, in the shadowiest recesses of my brain. Something I knew. Something I was missing.

I pulled out my notebook, turned to a fresh page, and started again from the beginning.

36

Y ou were different from all the others who came before you. You made me realise how I chose, and that fascinated me. I was so thrilled, so excited by the possibilities that this new understanding of myself opened up, that I nearly started to tell you all about it.

You had already poured your own breakfast coffee when I arrived. It was clear I was disturbing a relaxed, weekend breakfast, but you were polite enough to pretend I was welcome.

I knew there wasn't much time. I'd seen her leave for her run a few minutes earlier, and I suspected she didn't have true endurance. Her running outfit was a little too shiny, her shoes a little fluorescent to suggest a true athlete. She would jog around for perhaps as little as twenty minutes, rarely close to sweating or even mussing her hair, then she would soak in a bath for an hour and consider it well deserved.

Of course, it turned out that I underestimated her stamina by quite a bit, but I didn't know that at the time.

I asked for milk for my coffee. You turned to the fridge to get it and I slipped the pills into your half-drunk coffee. That was another risk. A full cup only just diluted the chalky taste of the

*pills. I held my breath as you returned to the counter, took a gulp
of your coffee and made a face.*

*You commented that it tasted funny. I could hear my own
heartbeat echo urgently in my ears as I sipped my own and said
it seemed fine to me. You shrugged, said caffeine was caffeine and
gulped the rest then you sat down quite suddenly, your eyes
already hazy. I was thrilled.*

*In seconds you were out. I tipped my coffee away — regret-
fully, it was a rich Brazilian roast — washed and dried my cup
carefully, then replaced it in the cupboard in the exact same spot
I'd watched you take it from minutes earlier. I doubted she would
noticed a single cup slightly out of place in the midst of what she
would return to, but I learned a long time ago that no chance was
worth taking.*

*It wasn't difficult to slip the pill bottle into your hand. I was
wearing gloves, of course. I'd slipped them off when you opened
the door, and had been careful to touch nothing but the cup, tap
and cupboard handle, all of which I wiped before I left. You had
been still the entire time I had been stealthily moving around the
kitchen, making sure that everything was impeccable. I wondered
if you were dead yet.*

*The pills were new to me: a combination of a higher dosage of
the SNRIs you had been prescribed for your pain, with a just little
sprinkling of my special ingredient. I had an idea of how quickly
they would take effect, but I was curious to find out.*

*Testing was, for obvious reasons, limited. I had trapped a pair
of rats years before and they dutifully multiplied for me, but
outside of lab conditions I could never be quite as confident of
precise results as I would like to be. It was frustrating.*

*I pressed my gloved fingers to the side of your neck. Nothing.
You were gone.*

Your weakness had been eradicated from the world.

37

'I don't know what to say, Ellie. They should have told you.'

Mia's eyes were troubled as she reached forward and gave me a hug. I'd waited outside their flat for her to come down. I was afraid to see Krister, certain that he would take one look at me and guess everything I had worked out. So I had texted Mia to ask if she would come for a walk with me.

She wrapped a brightly coloured shawl around her shoulders, slipped her arm through mine, and steered me through the early evening crowds. The sun was low, bathing everything in the other worldly glow of dusk. I felt curiously detached from her, from everything in fact, almost as though I were in a dream.

'Liv was afraid it would be difficult for you to be relaxed with her if you knew their whole history before you even met, but she still thought you should know. She hoped you would understand. It was Johan.' Mia broke off, shook her head. 'He is such an idiot sometimes. He kept promising he would tell you everything soon, then every time it was not yet the right time. They have been fighting about it all summer.'

I nodded, the dull ache of tension in my jaw. The low evening sun shone in my eyes as we walked down Folkunga-gatan towards the ferry terminal. 'Did you all discuss it?' I asked. 'Have you all been strategising when and how to break the news to poor Ellie?'

'No — no, of course — it was not like that. Liv has been so upset —'

I turned away.

'Johan loves you,' Mia insisted. 'I know he is too stupid to show it properly sometimes, but I told you he is the happiest he has ever been with you, and I meant it. Please don't do anything too hasty, Ellie. As Johan's friend, and as your friend — I hope. I don't have the right to ask you to give him more patience, I can only say that I think it would be worth it.'

'Yeah,' I muttered. My voice sounded distant and faraway in my own ears. 'Yeah, maybe.'

We crossed the road at the far end of the island and started to climb the little wooden stairs cut into the hill beyond. Mia had let go of my arm as the steps were narrow in places, but she was right behind me. My feet were surprisingly steady as we made our way to the top of the hill. We passed a handful of early evening picnickers here and there. A group of teenagers passed a box of wine between them. A woman watched the sunset while her boyfriend sat next to her, engrossed in his phone. A young dad photographed his toddler examining a weed growing between the rocks.

At the top of the hill, the city was laid out below us, the deep blue water of the harbour twinkling in the evening sun, the little matchstick roofs and steeples of Gamla Stan almost silhouetted. I noticed a few dark clouds gathering in the distance.

'Liv agrees with me,' Mia insisted. 'We have discussed many times how you are good for Johan, how you make him happy. She knows better than anyone how difficult he can be. I think she would be a good friend to you if you let her.'

'How long were they together?'

'Fifteen years. From when they were sixteen until a little more than two years ago.'

A lifetime. I could barely conceive of knowing someone that long.

The dark clouds I'd seen had rolled in. They brooded above the Stockholm skyline, low and menacing. A storm had been predicted earlier that day, I remembered dully. The air zinged with electricity as darkness rolled over the city. The dad wrestled the toddler into one of those hiking backpacks, the baby howling its protest at being separated from its precious weed.

'And was it his getting into punch ups and stuff that split them up?'

'They made an agreement to keep it private, but yes, I think so. She tried as long as she could to help him but in the end she didn't know how.'

'He's talking about going in to therapy.'

'That is great.'

'So then maybe they can get back together.'

'Ellie, no. That isn't what I meant. They split up for so many reasons, I'm sure.'

'Name another one.'

'I — I don't know, but —'

'Did Sanna know about them?'

'I think so, yes.'

'They didn't keep it a secret from her?'

'I don't know. She might have already known from someone else. They all know many of the same people. People used to talk about Johan and Liv, because it was so amazing, a teenage couple staying together so long. Sanna could have heard about them from lots of people.'

I nodded and turned away. There was a Swedish flag at the top of the hill behind us. I could hear it rattling in the wind.

'Ellie, please, talk to Johan, at least let him explain —'

'Did you know that Gustav Lindström, Sanna's ex boyfriend was murdered?'

'What?' I could hear the shock in Mia's voice. A little boat made its way out to sea far below us, black against the inky purple water. The wind whipped up white tipped waves rippling across the harbour. A little shiver of terror rattled through me.

'Gustav Lindström had a heart attack,' Mia said.

'A heart attack someone caused. Maybe the same person who killed Sanna.' I turned to look at her. She was staring at me, her eyes wide with horror.

And maybe fear. *Did she know,* I wondered. Did she suspect?

'Ellie, I think maybe you need to —'

'I'm going home,' I said. 'To London. Maybe just for a break, maybe forever. I'm not sure yet.'

Mia didn't say anything. A chilly breeze danced under my collar, and I shivered. The sun slipped below the horizon.

'I understand,' she said finally. 'I wish you would stay, but I understand. I will explain to Johan.'

I nodded. 'There's just something I have to do, then I've got a flight booked early tomorrow.'

'Would you like to stay with us tonight?'

'No I — I have another friend I'm going to stay with. Thanks, though.'

'What is it you need to do? Something more about Sanna?'

I looked away, pins and needles nipping at my fingers. 'Something like that. I've found something out that I need to tell the police. And then I'll go.'

'Ellie are you sure that is a good idea? How could you know something the police don't?'

I shrugged. 'Maybe I don't. Maybe I'm completely wrong. That's for them to figure out.'

'Can I drive you to the airport?'

'I'll be fine. Thank you.'

'I wish things could be different.'

'So do I.'

The first thick raindrops splattered the rocks and the heavens opened.

38

JOHAN

As the first shards of dawn broke across the grey sky, Johan finally admitted that Ellie was gone. He had hardly slept, had tossed and turned, listening to the summer storm raging outside, fumbling for his phone every few minutes to check for messages. He must have dropped off at some point, because he had woken, feeling groggy and queasy and vaguely discomfited from a series of troubling dreams.

She wasn't lying next to him. There was no sound of the kettle boiling, no shower running, or singing under her breath as she pottered about. Not that he was surprised, after Mia's call. He had just hoped.

From the moment he'd met Ellie, he'd hoped. He had taken one look at her freckly nose and wild hair and sparkling eyes and he had hoped. Had held his breath and crossed his fingers for one more day, one more moment with her before she saw him for what he was and he lost her.

At least she hadn't packed everything, he thought. She wasn't completely gone. Her lotions and potions had still been cluttered around the bathroom sink the night before.

He could see her trainers strewn in front of the door, the armchair piled high with discarded clothes, the celebrity gossip magazines in English and Swedish covering the bedside table. Whenever Ellie caught him glancing at her mess, she'd quickly swear she was just about to tidy up, but he didn't mind it at all. He was just happy it meant she was there.

So she must be coming back, at least briefly. He rolled onto his back and stared at the ceiling, a wave of misery washing over him as he caught the scent of Ellie from her pillow. Her citrusy shampoo, coconut body lotion and something else that was indefinably her.

Maybe when she came to pack, they could talk. Maybe, somehow, he could explain. Make her see, make her understand that it was never about lying to her, it was —

It was what?

It was about lying to her.

It was about the lie that he deserved her.

Johan fucked up. It was what he did. He disappointed people. Since the moment he was born, he had had a vague sense that there was something not quite right about him, an inkling that he wasn't quite the one his parents ordered. He wasn't enough or he was too much, he wasn't sure which. All he knew was that whatever he was it was wrong. It was no one's fault, it was just how it was. He tried not to think about it.

When he was little, he imagined a hole inside of himself, like a jigsaw piece missing. He managed to answer questions in class fairly often. He learned to make the other kids laugh, and some of them became his friends. He never caused extra work for his mother if he could help it and he kept out of his father's way. It was just that the one little jigsaw piece that would have tied it all together, made him a proper person, had been lost somewhere along the way.

As he got older, the hole became a void and he knew that if he so much as looked in its direction, it would suck him in. So he didn't. He plastered over the hole with beer and fights and being the loudest, funniest person anyone had ever met. Liv let him kiss her at Lasse Beckman's sixteenth birthday party. It was summer but it was late at night and cold and he still remembered his surprise at how warm her lips were. The relief that crashed over him. The hope that maybe if Liv thought he was normal, then it was almost true.

Of course the therapist his mother made him go to after his father was found on Folkungagatan told him that none of it was his fault. Of course she did. It was her job to try to make him feel better. Johan understood, in an abstract way, that there was nothing a small child could do to stop his parents being so unhappy, but it didn't change the fact that Johan was broken. Just because you're paranoid doesn't mean they aren't out to get you.

Johan got up, toyed with his phone as he waited for the coffee machine to heat up. Should he text Ellie or give her some space? Mia said she was distraught about him and Liv. The thought tore at him, ragged nails scratching at his heart. He would leave it for now. Wait until she came home to get her things.

Liv stayed with him for years after their relationship had run its course because she was afraid he wouldn't manage on his own. He could still remember the sting of mortification that prickled over him when she admitted that, a year after their split. He'd wanted to turn himself inside out with shame. Instead he'd gone out that night and come home with Sanna.

Sanna was beautiful, charming, interesting when she felt like it, but they were never suited. They weren't supposed to be. It had amused her to slum it from her usual actors, musicians, start up millionaires for a summer and being with her helped him persuade Liv that he was just fine and she could get on with her life.

It had been fun, to begin with, but as the bickering increased Johan felt himself start to crumble. Even once he realised that Sanna enjoyed those arguments, that she would say cutting things just to wind him up for fun, it still frightened him.

By September, he was craving the weekend at Krister's cottage. Just to be with his friends, to relax and breathe, and prepare for the conversation that was waiting for him back in Stockholm. Then she showed up at Sturekajen as he and Liv boarded the ferry on the Friday evening. *Hej hej! Surprise!* He'd stared at her coldly then got on the ferry and sat by himself, freezing on the top deck.

Liv came up the stairs just as they pulled out of Vaxholm, demanded to know why the hell he was being such an asshole. He'd tried to explain that he and Sanna had specifically agreed she would stay home for the weekend, that they would give each other a break and talk the following week. Liv snapped that Sanna was there now, so he had to pull himself together and stop being such a child. He had meekly gone down and apologised, but he was still angry. Why did she have to come when she knew they would only fight?

He hadn't even absorbed the horror of her death when Krister broke it to him that a newspaper had accused him of her murder. Krister had begged Johan not to read it, not to read any of it, advising him to keep his head down, ignore it all and wait for the storm to blow over. Krister knew a bit about dealing with media storms from his job working with controversial drugs, so Johan took his advice and hid from the world for weeks and weeks.

He'd lied to Ellie about that. It wasn't that his old friends looked at him with suspicion in their eyes. It was that he was afraid to look at them in case he saw it.

When Ellie tripped over him on the beach that night, it was like a fresh start. There were no question marks in her eyes when she looked at him. No sympathy about his father, no pity that Liv thought she had to sacrifice herself for him. No frown, no dart of nerves, no faltering smile as though she knew that Sanna Johansson dumped him hours before her death, and so had Karin Söderstrom.

I never would have predicted you becoming one of them. I've never killed anyone I knew before, unless you count Karin but I didn't really know her. There wasn't anything of her to know. She was a wisp, a ghost, a shadow of a person, like a seedling that sprouts the tiniest shoot then simply shrivels up for no reason.

That's what they all are. Weak. Pathetic. Inadequate. Helping them to shrivel is my gift to them, to those around them, to the world at large. I should be celebrated, thanked, lauded. Awarded prizes and grants and respect for having the strength to allow natural selection to flourish. It is the medical establishment, the government, the social services who are cruelly contemptible, destroying the human race by allowing the feeble to thrive as parasites.

You hid your weakness well. I give you full credit for that. You almost fooled even me.

Sanna Johansson, the Queen of the Night. Full of fun and laughter and adventure, followed by a trail of gossip wherever she went. Modelling contracts, famous boyfriends, offers for a residency at a Los Angeles club. But that's all it was, wasn't it?

Whispers. A mirage, masking the scared little girl who had to pop pills just to leave her house and face the world every day.

When you confessed your true self, I nearly laughed. I'd already felt the urge around you many times, but I have standards. I don't kill just because I don't like someone; that would make me pathetic. I had worried, even, that the urge was getting stronger, more indiscriminate. That I was finally turning into the monster I had always feared I was.

But I should have trusted myself. I should have known that my instincts are never wrong. You were one of my special people all along. It hardly took any persuasion to talk you into coming to the cottage that weekend with us after all. 'He really wants you there. He won't admit it — you know what he's like — but I know how much you mean to him.'

You lapped it up like the pathetic narcissist you were.

This is how I know I am developing. From the messy terror of Karin to the exquisitely timed certainty of you, I've learned and improved and honed and refined. The tragedy is that it's unlikely anyone will ever know.

People's minds are too narrow to ever put aside the absurdities we teach our children and appreciate the reality of life. I blame education. It is ridiculous to teach children Darwin in one lesson, then in the very next period claim them the very opposite in Ethics or whatever nonsense they are calling it these days.

We are so proud of being so liberal, so accepting, it's disgusting. The most tolerant country in the world? I alone expose the lie of that.

Gustav was a mistake. I fully admit it.

It was just the way he was sobbing like a child, I couldn't stand it.

All the same, it was impulsive, hasty, ill considered.

It was unworthy of me.

It was her fault.

As a rule, I do not believe in blaming others for my failings. That is a sign of weakness. But she is a special case.

She is a true adversary.

And very soon, she will know it.

If she doesn't already.

'So you're the famous Johan.'

Ellie's friend Maddie gave Johan the kind of cool, even gaze that normally made him squirm, but he barely registered it now. Ellie hadn't answered her phone in over a day, nor had she shown up to pick up a change of clothes or her toothbrush. His messages to her were undelivered. After another sleepless night, he remembered Ellie mentioning the regular coffee morning at Café String, so he had called in sick and waited for Maddie outside.

'Have you been in touch with Ellie?' he demanded.

'See you next time Maddie!' The rest of the newcomers coffee group filed out of the cafe. Maddie gave them a distracted wave as she stared at Johan with troubled eyes.

'Since when?'

'Since Tuesday night.'

'Nearly two days? She hasn't been home in all that time?'

'I hoped she was staying with you. My friend Mia said she was planning to go back to London but she has not packed or taken any of her things.'

'Did she have it out with you about not telling her about you and Liv?'

He shook his head. 'I haven't seen her since she found out. But she met Mia and they talked. Mia said Ellie was too upset to talk to me yet, and that she would stay with a friend. I thought that would be you. I was waiting until she got home to try to —' He shrugged helplessly. 'I don't know. Beg her to understand.'

'You're an idiot,' Maddie said with a sad smile.

'I know.'

Maddie frowned. 'Let me try calling her. She might answer if it's me.'

Johan felt his stomach twist with nerves as Maddie put the phone to her ear and frowned. *Please let her answer*. Even if it meant she was avoiding him, at least he would know she was okay. Maddie shook her head. 'Straight to voicemail. Her phone is off or out of service.'

'It's been like that for almost a day and a half.'

'Ellie didn't reply to my texts yesterday, but I just figured she'd got caught up in stuff.' Maddie opened up her message app, her eyes worried. 'They've not been delivered. I don't think she would have got on a plane without saying anything to me. And even if she did, it's only a couple of hours to London, she'd be back in service by now. You don't have one of those stalk-your-partner apps, do you?'

'What?'

'You know, the ones where you can see where your friends' phones are, but everyone knows they're really to keep tabs on your other half?'

Johan shook his head.

'Let me ring Lena, she might have some ideas, or know whether we should call the police yet. Hold on.'

Maddie stepped away. Johan leaned against one of the

tables outside the café. Despite the storm the night before, the clouds were still low and heavy, brooding over the city, making the mid morning feel like dusk. The hollow feeling was growing inside Johan's chest.

Sanna. Karin.

Ellie.

No. Not Ellie. Please not Ellie, he begged silently.

He felt a numb panic gnawing at him. He should be frantic. He was frantic, inside. He should be shouting and yelling, finding her, saving her. But he felt frozen. It was like the time when he was little, and had been kicking a ball around Mariatorget when it rolled into the main road and he ran after it. He heard the urgent blast of the car horn echo in his ears as though from far away, but he couldn't move.

Could only watch, trapped, terror sliding through his veins like acid as the blue car came closer and closer, filling his vision. *This is what happened to Daddy. This is what happened to Daddy.* Then the man who ran the ice cream stand yanked his arm and he was back on the pavement and the man was shouting at his mother and she was screaming, holding him close, and the blue car kept going.

'Lena says we should go to the police,' Maddie said, and Johan nodded. 'She said we should go there in person, ask to speak to the team that interviewed Ellie last week. She's texting me their names.'

'Who — what? The police interviewed her last week?'

Johan stared at Maddie in shock, chills scuttling down his spine.

Maddie shook her head. 'Oh Ellie, for fuck's sake. Come on. I'll fill you in on the way.'

41

JOHAN

A man had been killed after arguing with Ellie. Some guy who used to date Sanna — what on earth had Ellie been talking to him about? Gustav someone or other. The name rang a vague bell. Sanna had talked about him. She'd said something about him bothering her, but she had assured Johan it was under control.

Someone killed that guy? When Ellie was nearby? Because of Sanna? Johan's head was spinning.

Maddie had got on the T-bana at Mariatorget, reminding him again of his promise to contact her the instant he heard anything. 'And I'll call you right away if I do,' she added, biting her lip. 'Lena might be able to ask around her police contacts a bit, get the inside track. I don't know. She'll be alright.'

Johan nodded. The numb, hollow feeling was pressing on his lungs, his windpipe. His girlfriend was missing, he was supposed to be sad. *Just try not to be sad.*

'I don't think they're worried about her,' Maddie added. 'That's my gut feeling. They were interested, but they weren't concerned. I reckon they think she's hiding out somewhere, taking a break from everything, just getting her head together.'

'Where would she be? She doesn't know anyone in Sweden except me and you.'

Maddie rubbed his arm. 'I think it if we've learned anything today, it's that Ellie's been up to a lot more than either of us knew. Who knows who else she knows. She's a smart girl. She knows how to take care of herself.'

But her forced smile told him she didn't believe it any more than he did. 'I'll ring soon, okay?' She gave him a quick hug and disappeared into the station, leaving Johan alone.

He should go home. Ellie could be there, waiting for him, munching on cereal because she couldn't be bothered waiting for dinner. He checked his phone again, but there was nothing, of course. His messages to her were still undelivered. She was still gone.

He couldn't bear the thought of sitting in the flat without her. He needed to take action, to do something, anything, to find her, to make sure she was safe. He just didn't know what. He'd tried ringing Krister earlier but he hadn't answered, and neither had Mia. Mia had a big event on that night, and Krister would probably be locked away in the lab, working for hours, forgetting even to eat.

Once, at uni, Krister had collapsed from dehydration after working without so much as a sip of water for a full day during a heat wave. He had told them all that evening, with a bizarre pride, as though damaging himself was a badge of honour. Johan, almost qualified as a nurse, had started to lecture him, and Liv had laughed and called him an idiot, but Mia had been angry.

When Johan and Liv left Krister's student room that night and were walking hand-in-hand back to the T-bana,

Liv had turned to Johan, her eyes shining. *Mia was in to Krister — it was so obvious!*

It was going to be so perfect. Four best friends, all in love. Johan had shaken his head, said he thought four best friends in love was a bit weird if anything. Liv laughed and called him an old cynic.

It didn't quite work out like that in any case, Johan thought. He and Liv had only had a couple of good years left in them at that point, and though Krister had never said outright, Johan often suspected that all wasn't entirely well between him and Mia. Once, months ago now, before Ellie arrived, they'd all been having dinner at a Thai place near Skantstull. Liv had been held up at work, and when Johan got there, Krister and Mia were already at the table. They didn't see him, and Johan had hesitated by the door a moment, unsure as to what he was looking at.

They were sitting, side by side, staring into space, in silence. As though they were unaware of one another's presence. As though they were robots put on pause.

Seconds later, Liv arrived in a flurry of apologies and complaints about her boss. Mia had jumped up to greet them both and Johan decided it couldn't have been as odd as it looked. Krister and Mia lived together, worked together some of the time. They'd probably just run out of things to say.

Johan found himself outside Liv's apartment building before he realised. He hadn't rung her that morning when he rang Krister and Mia. He had started to dial, automatically reaching out to Liv for comfort and advice like he always did, but then he had remembered Mia describing Ellie's distress.

Things were long over with Liv, if they'd ever really existed. They'd been kids. Best friends playing at being in love without really knowing what it meant, then best friends who loved each other deeply but had no idea how to be adults together. Now, finally, they were just best friends and it was perfect.

But Ellie didn't see it that way. How could she, when she didn't know any of it? The thought of her feeling hurt and threatened and as though he didn't love her tore Johan up inside. He couldn't believe he had been so stupid. He'd thought he was protecting Ellie by waiting until the right moment to tell her everything, but all he'd done was upset her.

Johan punched in the code for Liv's building and took the stairs two at a time.

'Liv!' he bellowed at her front door. She hadn't answered when he rang the doorbell, but that wasn't unusual, she normally ignored it if she wasn't expecting anyone. Unexpected calls turned out often than not to be neighbours, members of the residents' association board trying to drum up support for some hostile coup or other.

'Are you home?' Johan yelled.

Liv's flat was in silence, the hallway unusually shadowy. She must have closed her living room blinds, Johan thought in surprise. That wasn't like her.

She mustn't be home. If she was there, there would be music on, or TV, or probably both. When they lived together, the constant background noise had driven Johan bonkers.

He stepped back into the hallway and was about to lock the door behind him when he stopped. Liv should be home by now. She was an early bird, at the gym by 6am, office by 7:30, because she loved nothing more than long evenings relaxing at home, or with friends. He looked at his watch. Quarter to six. He knew Liv. He couldn't think of a single occasion on which Liv hadn't been home at a quarter to six.

His heart beginning to thud, a strange, echoing sound in his ears, Johan opened the door again, stepped into her dimly lit hallway. He closed it carefully behind him, feeling a strange impulse to protect Liv from preying eyes. She might be ill. She could have picked up a summer cold, or a migraine. She might be in such a deep sleep she hadn't heard his shout.

Not bothering to take his shoes off, Johan walked slowly down the long hallway. Liv's bedroom door was open. Her bed was neatly made as usual, no sign of her there. The kitchen was empty. He finally made it to the living room and paused, his blood roaring in his ears as his brain tried to register and reject the sight.

She was asleep. She was asleep, she was asleep. His mind frantically, urgently, pleaded with him even as he felt a howl building in his chest. She was lying face down on the floor, her knees bent at an awkward angle under her, almost as though she had been looking for something under the sofa and had just stopped.

Nej, nej nej, Liv — snälla —

Johan wasn't sure whether he moaned the words out loud as he sank to his knees. His whole body shook as he leaned forward and gently brushed Liv's hair back from her face. Her eyes were wide and staring. The scream that ricocheted around the room was his.

42

JOHAN

Someone must have handed Johan a cup of coffee at some point because he now held one in his hands. He was sitting on the stairs opposite Liv's front door, watching police swarm in and out of her flat. Radios crackled static, detectives conferred in low voices, and from deep inside the flat flashbulbs went off as every inch of Liv's home was photographed and dusted, analysed and swept for fibres.

She would hate that, Johan thought dully. Liv wasn't a neat freak like him, but she didn't like other people touching her stuff. She used to say it came from being the eldest of five, that she had had a lifetime of younger siblings' grubby fingers ruining her precious things and she wasn't putting up with it as an adult. Johan felt a dry sob shudder through him. Her parents and siblings. Someone must have contacted them, but he should talk to them. They would need to hear from him.

He was hunched over, one arm wrapped around his waist as though physically holding himself together. The hollow feeling wasn't even there. There was nothing. Johan looked in surprise at the cup of coffee he was holding. He took a sip. It was cold and bitter and his hand was trembling.

There was a uniformed officer, a young guy with a shaved head, watching him intently as though trying to decipher something. Guarding him? Did a person who had just lost their best friend drink coffee? Johan wondered. Should he be doing something deeper, more impassioned. Howling, screaming, singing a lament of abject grief.

Just try not to be sad.

What should I do? The plea rattled around his head. *Tell me how I am supposed to be.*

He took another sip of the rancid coffee, grimaced and put it down on the stair. He leaned against the landing, feeling the wall cool against his temple as he stared blindly at the floor. He could hear rasping, gurgling, uneven breathing coming from somewhere, and after a moment he realised it was him.

Liv.

Somewhere, in some distant place, memories were playing incessantly, like on an old fashioned projector, flickering through his mind. The first time he saw her, she had been giving a speech to the school about the need to save dolphins from the tuna fishing industry. She'd been so forceful, so passionate, so certain of herself and her convictions. Johan had been dazzled, in awe of her for years.

The night they kissed at Lasse Beckman's party. He'd reached out to stroke her hair and she had moved at the last second so he accidentally brushed her breast. He had been mortified, stuttering terrified apologies, swearing he hadn't meant it. She'd laughed and said he could touch it if he wanted to and Johan had been fairly sure what he felt in that moment was the pinnacle of human happiness.

The day they moved into their first apartment when he'd

tried to carry her over the threshold then tripped and they'd both gone flying, collapsing in the hallway in a fit of giggles.

Liv. Liv was dead. However hard he tried, he couldn't get the words to mean anything.

Two plain clothed officers, a dark haired woman and a man with salt and pepper hair stood in Liv's doorway talking in low voices. Johan recognised them. The detectives. They had come to the island, when Ellie found Sanna's body.

And today. He had met them at the police station. Was that just today? When he and Maddie reported Ellie missing.

Ellie was missing.

The detectives had questioned Ellie. Last week. And now they were here.

'Liv! What's happening — let me through — I'm her best friend — Liv!'

The young officer darted forward to stop Mia as she screamed, flung herself towards Liv's door, snatching at the crime scene tape blocking her way.

'Nej nej nej nej —' Mia's howls echoed around the walls. She fought the young officer, elbowing him in the chest, kicking at his shins, screeching Liv's name over and over.

'Please, please calm down.' Johan heard the young officer's low, gentle voice as he held Mia tightly. 'Just breathe for a moment. Breathe with me, slowly.'

After a moment Mia's wails softened into ragged, gasping sobs.

That's how you do it, thought Johan dully. That's how I am supposed to be. But still he felt only the abyss.

'It's not true,' Mia muttered. 'It's not true.'

'Just keep breathing,' the officer said.

'Not her. Not Liv. Please not Liv.'

Please not Liv, thought Johan.

'Where is Ellie?' Mia demanded suddenly. Her eyes flew open and she stared accusingly at Johan. 'Where is Ellie?'

Johan opened his mouth to say that he didn't know, and Mia's face crumpled.

'No — no, it's not true — it can't be true. Where is she Johan? What did she do? What did you let her do?'

43

I t was the end of winter, around Easter time. Filthy snow was piled everywhere and the slush of melting ice was ankle deep on the pavements. The stink of a whole winter's worth of dog piss now released by the thaw was everywhere, and I wrapped my scarf over my nose as I splashed through puddles.

I wasn't going anywhere in particular. It was too dark and cold to do anything but wander around and see what there was to see. My parents hadn't even noticed when I slipped out. They were so engrossed in some stupid game show that they didn't even look up when I walked past them in full outdoor gear and closed our apartment door behind me.

Walking around the city by night was my favourite thing to do. Once, I even crossed Slussen into Gamla Stan, but the narrow little alleyways and crooked buildings that looked as though witches might reach out the windows and grab children frightened me, so I had scuttled back through the underpass. Some older kids — almost adults, but not quite, had been hanging about outside that night club and they shouted to me, told me I was too young to be out alone at this time. I ignored them and kept running until I reached Götgatan.

It wasn't until I drowned the cat that I felt better.

It was easy. I walked all the way along Götgatan to the very end, and then to the canal. It had been frozen for some of winter and people had skated on it, but now the ice was all broken up and floating about in chunks.

I didn't have to wait very long until a cat came along. It might have been a stray or an adventurous pet, I don't know. It was friendly, so it was probably used to people. It let me pick it up and it didn't even yowl until it was mid air, right before it plunged into the water. The stupid thing didn't realise what was happening when I first threw it.

It was just a few nights later that I was hanging about Björnsträdgården, watching some drunk idiots play on a broken guitar, when I spotted someone who looked familiar. At first, I thought he was one of the usual drunks, but he looked a little bit more smartly dressed. He clearly had a home, where there was a shower and a change of clothes. Interesting.

Then I realised he wasn't just familiar, I actually knew him. I had seen him at my school before. He was the father of one of the kids in my class. That quiet boy who hadn't known how to tie shoelaces on our first day, and spent most recesses playing football alone. I was intrigued. My own parents never touched alcohol, it hadn't occurred to me that other parents might. I was curious, so I followed him.

He went into a pub on Tjärhovsgatan which was quite boring because I couldn't even see him. I waited a few moments, then I was just about to give up and find something more interesting, when he staggered out again, around the corner towards Folkungagatan. He tried to get into one of the pubs there, but there was a man at the door who pushed him back. They shouted a little, the father of the quiet boy getting quite red faced and angry, but the other man held firm and eventually he walked on.

When he got to Götgatan, he crossed the road and started to wander towards the entrance of the new tunnel. I had been in the tunnel, in a car with my parents, but I had no idea people could walk in it. I was excited. I could hear the strange, echoing zooms of cars zipping by. There weren't many at that time of night, but it was a thrilling sound.

The sidewalk stopped, because maybe people weren't supposed to walk in there, and the man hesitated as though he had decided it was a bad idea. I was disappointed. To have come so close for him just to turn away like a grown up. It made me angry. It made me hate him.

Then I thought of something. I bet if I ran down there, he would follow. He was a grown up, a parent, even. That was the sort of thing they did.

He was already backing away. There wasn't much time. I started to run, heard his shout echo in my ear as I raced past him. I risked a glance behind me. To my joy he was chasing me, but he was lumbering and confused, lurching this way and that as I zipped back and forth, keeping just out his grasp.

He never saw the van coming, but I did. My heart began to beat faster with excitement. I knew what was going to happen. And then it happened.

The horn and the screech of tires were exciting, the roar of the engine bouncing all around the tunnel as the van sped away was interesting. But I was disappointed by the thud the man's body made when it slammed onto the tarmac. It wasn't really anything. I thought it would be much louder, that I would be able to hear bones breaking and things.

I crept closer. There was a lot of blood around him, and his breathing sounded strange and gurgly, but he opened his eyes.

'Don't be afraid,' he said. His voice sounded like when I blew milk bubbles through a straw and my mother shouted at me. 'It's okay. I'll be okay. I just need you to go and shout for help, okay? A *policeman if you can find one, but any adult. Just go and shout as loud as you can.'*

I frowned. Why would I do that? Adults ruined fun things.

'I know you, don't I? You go to the same school as my Johan. You're his friend, aren't you?'

I didn't understand why everyone kept talking to me about friends. Why don't you have any friends? You should make friends. Try not to worry about not having friends. I didn't even know what a friend was. Why would I want one?

And now this man was telling me that the boy who couldn't tie shoelaces was my friend. Maybe that was interesting. At least I knew what to say the next time my mother cried about me not having friends.

I got bored then, and walked away. I could hear the man's voice behind me as I ran back up the little road that led back out into the air. 'That's it. Well done. Just shout for any adult. You're doing a great job!'

When the boy Johan came back to school a few weeks later, I asked him why he was so sad and he told me that his father had died.

'Why does that make you sad?'

'I don't know. It just does.'

'Well you should just not be sad.'

'I will try.'

'Do you want to play? Do you know about Pokémon?'

He nodded and we started to play and my mother never cried about my lack of friends again.

Little did I know then how important the man in the tunnel really was.

Many, many years later, it was Johan who mentioned he was working on a clinical trial for a new heart medication. I knew immediately that it was too close to my special ingredient, that if the drug was approved it would begin to show up in tests. I went to surprise Johan at work.

He looked pale and drawn, as though drained of blood. Was he ill? Oh yes — her. Sanna. He was sad again.

'Let me take you to lunch.'

'I'm not really in the mood.'

'Hey. You should try not to be sad.'

He smiled, a strange, haunted smile. 'I will try.'

'Come on. My treat.'

He nodded distractedly and when we were in the corridor I pretended I'd left my phone in the office. It didn't take me two seconds to alter a couple of results. Barely noticeable, just enough to throw the trial into question and put the drug back years.

When they accused Johan he didn't even remember I'd been there that day.

44

The sky was as dark as night as the ferry lurched violently from side to side. I'd long given up on pretending I was okay. I sat in the centre aisle, bent double, my nose pressed into my knees, frantically counting to ten backwards and forwards and moaning whenever the wind shrieked.

It was safe, I told myself, over and over. It had to be. They wouldn't keep going if it wasn't.

A fresh gust of rain battered against the windows and the engine juddered as though something was trapped in it. Terror churned in my guts and I wanted to cry. An older couple were playing cards at the booth next to me, laughing heartily as though we weren't being tossed about like an empty coke can.

I knew there was a storm coming. I'd seen it gathering when I talked to Mia. I shouldn't have run for the last ferry, I should have waited until morning.

Morning would have been too late.

The captain made an announcement over the loud-speaker, for all I knew, telling us all we were about to die.

That said, we seemed to be rocking ever so slightly less, enough that I forced myself to uncurl to a sitting position and looked around. It was too dark to see much outside, but the rain rattling against the window sounded lighter. Every other passenger was happily going about their business. Playing cards, reading, amusing sleepy children.

My hands were shaking, pins and needles nipping at my fingers and my heart seemed determined to break free of my rib cage. We had to be nearly there. It couldn't be much longer.

I closed my eyes and thought of Johan. The last time we were on this ferry, he'd thought I'd dropped off, had absent-mindedly played with my hair while he watched football on his phone. I remembered feeling his breath warm on my hair when he kissed the top of my head, even though he thought I was fast asleep. I'd felt safe.

The ferry pulled up at the little jetty and I staggered off on shaking legs. It was almost full dark, and a light rain splattered the now mercifully still sea. The moon came out from behind a cloud and I spotted Krister's boat tied to a post.

45

Something was screaming in Johan's head and he couldn't figure it out. Something was wrong. Something was very wrong. Of course it was — Liv was dead. But it wasn't that. Johan saw his hand move and for a second he was surprised it was still there. He felt so detached from everything, even himself. He didn't know if he was hot or cold or hungry or full.

He just knew that everything was wrong.

'Some jealousy is natural of course, but —' Mia hesitated, glanced over at him with regret in her eyes. She reached over to touch Johan's arm, but he didn't move. 'I'm so sorry, I hate saying this, but I don't think Ellie's behaviour has been normal.'

'Can you be more specific?' The female detective, Nadja, leaned forward, her pen poised. The odd thought flickered across Johan's mind that she didn't seem to like Mia, but that didn't make sense. Henrik, the other detective, was sitting back in his seat, watching the exchange.

They were in the coffee shop below Liv's apartment building. Police cars lined the street outside, crime scene tape blocked off the entrance to the building. Irritated pedestrians were stepping into the street to pass without crossing the road, and Johan could just see a woman he recognised as Liv's neighbour argue with the tall police officer guarding the door.

'Ellie came to Sanna's funeral, though of course she didn't know her. They had never even met. She claimed that it was out of respect, because she was the one who found the body, but then she wouldn't stop asking questions, about who everyone was, how well they knew Sanna. It felt like more than just curiosity, but I couldn't understand it. Then she started asking about Johan and Sanna, whether they were happy, why they split up.'

'What did you tell her?' Henrik asked.

Mia shrugged. 'I said I didn't really know. That's not the sort of thing Johan and I talk about it. And Krister wouldn't break his confidence, not even to me.'

'Was Ellie satisfied with this response?'

'Not at all,' Mia said with a sigh. 'I've been hearing for weeks how she has been going around all of our friends asking neverending questions. I've tried to reassure people as much as I can, but to be honest, they are finding her disturbing.'

'Could you write down the names of these other friends she spoke to?'

'Yes, of course. Linda Andersson was one, and of course you know about Gustav Lindström. I was there with her that night. I saw the way she stared at him in the bar. She must have approached him when I left her.'

Mia's words pierced through the fog cloaking Johan's mind. 'No, wait — you and Ellie had a drink together? When was this?' He couldn't quite grasp what Mia was saying. Something about Ellie talking to his friends. What was wrong with that? Nothing made sense in a world without Liv.

'I'm sorry Johan, I hate having to tell you this, but I can't protect her any more, when —'

A sob overcame Mia and her face crumpled. Johan automatically reached out and put his arm around her. The detectives waited until Mia had composed herself.

'Ellie told Johan that she was meeting some friends from her newcomers to Sweden club,' she said finally, in a low voice, 'but instead she met me, at Ugglan. I thought she wanted to talk to me, just to get to know me better, or maybe talk about Johan, the usual stuff, you know — but it became clear it was only a cover for her to watch Gustav. After I read about his death I noticed that he had accepted a new friend the day he died. Look —' She handed her phone to Nadja. 'She looks very different, but I'm sure that is Ellie.'

The two detectives glanced at Mia's phone then exchanged a look. 'Why do you think she might have set up a fake account to connect with Gustav Lindström?' Nadja asked.

'She was obsessed with your past, Johan. It was frightening. We all get a little bit curious about our partner's previous life, but Ellie has taken it so much further — do you know she visited our old school?'

'Our school? Why?'

'She had a meeting with Josefin Beckmann.'

Johan stared at her, trying to make sense of what she was saying. Ellie had met his high school history teacher?

'Johan, I think you have suspected—' Mia reached out, covered his hand with hers.

Johan shook his head, pulled his hand away. 'No — of course, I —'

'Why else did you not tell her the truth about you and Liv? I know it's difficult, but I think you know, deep down.'

'I — I was just worried —'

'You were worried she would go crazy,' Mia said gently. 'You knew she wouldn't be able to handle it.'

No, it wasn't like that. He had been worried, but not about Ellie's reaction. Not the way Mia was suggesting. He was sure of that. He shook his head, started to tell them that, to make sure the police understood that Ellie might have been hurt or worried — but not angry, not crazy.

But then an image of Liv's staring eyes assaulted him and a sob crashed over him and he couldn't say anything at all.

Once I managed to get the engine on, it turned out to be much like driving a car. If I didn't think too much about the fact that I was driving along on top of icy, inky-black water that was just waiting to welcome me to its depths. *There is a very deep channel that runs between two islands*, Johan had said. I must be crossing it about now.

I hadn't been able to figure out how to get the headlights on, assuming there even were headlights. At least the clouds had cleared following the storm and the moon was bright, bathing the islands all around me in an silver glow. Except for the tiny ripples the boat was making, the water was as still as glass.

The rumble of the engine sounded unnaturally loud amongst the silence, and I wished I could somehow muffle it as I made my way to trespass on Krister's property. Of course, I'd already nicked his boat, what was a spot of trespassing between friends?

A whisper of winter danced in the air as a chilly breeze lifted my hair. I shivered and turned the wheel as gently as I could towards the little cove where Krister had parked. I thought of Sanna out here alone, trapped under the ice for months on end.

My legs still felt wobbly, my hands slick with sweat on the worn, wooden steering wheel, but an eerie calm had stolen over me. It was as though my mind had narrowed, like the viewfinder in a par of binoculars, to a tiny pin prick focussed on only the task ahead of me. I knew what I had to do. I could worry about everything else later.

I cut the engine and let the gentle waves wash the boat towards the shore. Krister had stopped the boat a little away from the beach, I remembered, before it got too shallow, but I had no idea exactly where. The water was so dark I was too frightened to jump in in case it swallowed me hole. *Shit.* Why hadn't I thought of this? I nearly laughed. To have made it all this way from Stockholm by water only to get trapped a few metres from the shore.

I had taken a couple of swimming lessons, when I was little, I reminded myself. I crouched by the side of the boat where I'd jumped off before. Johan had already been standing in the water, a little over knee depth for him, and I'd clutched his hand, terrified even though I could see the rocky bottom twinkling in the sun. Now the darkness was impenetrable, and I had no way of knowing if I would land on rocks and scrape my bum or plunge into depths over my head.

Liquid fear nipped at my toes like nitrate. My heart wasn't racing any more, or maybe it was and I was too numb to feel it. A little wave hit a nearby rock and ricochetted back, causing the boat to rock and a sob of sheer terror rose up in me.

If the water was over my head I would die.

It was freezing cold and pitch black. My three lessons kicking along a foam board at the Tooting Bec Lido while my mum leapt about taking photos and cheering like a loon would be little match for that. I'd wash up next summer, I thought.

Johan's next fucking girlfriend would find me.

With a strangled scream, I tipped forward into the blackness.

'Do you remember the time she made us go swing dancing?' Krister asked, his voice hoarse. Krister and Mia were sitting on Johan's sofa, Johan belatedly realised he was sitting on Ellie's suitcase.

Johan felt his lips twitch into a smile at the memory. Liv had decided that it was important for a couple to have a hobby together. She'd then persuaded Mia of this, so Johan and Krister had found themselves at a club somewhere beneath Zinkensdamm, swiftly discovering that they appeared to have at least five left feet between them.

'I lost many toes that night,' Krister grinned, and raised his empty glass. His voice broke. 'To Liv.'

A wave of grief hit Johan like a train and took his breath away. For a moment, he couldn't speak, but raised his glass silently towards Krister. Mia didn't move.

'I know you're angry with me about what I said to the police,' she blurted.

Johan stared at the floor. 'No, not angry. It's just —' He sighed. He didn't know what it was *just*. He didn't know anything. He wanted to sleep but he was afraid to.

Mia got up abruptly and stood by the window. She stood in the semi-darkness, silhouetted by the fading sunlight, her spine almost unnaturally straight. She crossed her arms tightly around her, clutching onto the glass of snaps Krister had insisted on pouring them all to toast Liv.

'I was only trying to help,' Mia muttered.

'I know,' Johan said.

Krister was slumped back on the couch, drained, like a puppet cut loose from its strings. His eyes were alert, though, Johan noticed in surprise. He was watching Mia carefully, even though he wasn't looking directly at her.

Years ago, Johan and Liv were on holiday in Greece and they tried to adopt a stray cat. Or rather, Liv had tried to adopt a stray cat and Johan had followed along uncertainly, a bit worried about rabies but not wanting to disappoint her. Liv had tried to tempt it towards her with some tuna, and Johan remembered how it had crept forward, infinitesimally slowly, its eyes flicking between Liv and him, even as it focussed on the tuna. That's how Krister looked now, Johan realised, his mind foggy as he tried to understand what that meant.

That was how Krister always looked.

Even when they were all laughing and kidding around, when Krister was telling funny stories about his colleagues, he always had one eye on Mia. Watching for her reaction.

That night at the swing dancing, Johan had accidentally twirled Liv into the couple behind them, starting a domino effect of dancers crashing into one another. Krister and Mia were several couples behind them, and yet when Krister stumbled, Johan just glimpsed the look of cold fury Mia gave him.

Later, on the walk home, they had all swapped stories of how useless they'd been. Mia joined in the laughter, doing impressions of them all falling over one by one as Johan looked on in horror. Johan realised he must have imagined the look.

And in fact, Krister never talked about his colleagues any more, or about his work at all. Mia always stopped him, cut him off with a breezy eye roll about how no one wanted to hear stories about boring science stuff. Which was odd, because at university, Mia had studied the same science stuff as Krister. She had once been passionate about it.

Mia's phone buzzed and they all jumped. 'It might be the police,' Mia muttered, fumbling in her bag for it. She frowned at the number, then answered. 'Corinna?'

Johan watched as Mia paled. She stepped backwards, and for an instant Johan thought she would fall. He saw Krister tense as a shadow crossed Mia's expression.

'What is it? Is it about Ellie?' Johan demanded, but Mia ignored him. He and Krister both jumped when the door slammed behind her.

T he water was about waist deep, but the cold was so shocking I stumbled and fell to my knees, taking in a huge mouthful of icy sea. I spluttered, coughing frantically as I scrabbled to my feet. My head was above water, I could feel air, but I couldn't breathe it in —

I was gasping into emptiness, terror slamming me over and over as I flailed, screaming inside my head, until finally I coughed again and breathed in a lungful of sweet air.

I managed to stagger from the water and collapsed on the beach, barely feeling the pain of the rocks and pebbles against my knees as I took rasping, painful, breaths with freezing water lapping against my toes. When my breathing was almost normal again, punctuated by only the odd strangled cough, I sat down properly and saw that the boat had floated away. Well that was me committed then, I thought grimly as I made my shaky way up the path towards the cottage. I'd worry about Krister's boat later. Sorry Krister.

When the path evened out towards the top, I felt in my bag for the papers I'd copied from Corinna. Everything was soaked, but I'd tucked the print outs into the plastic wallet in my notebook, so they were almost unscathed by their dip into the Baltic Sea. The base on Krister's family's island had never been used. The Russians had known about it all along, according to a Soviet military log Corinna's team had uncovered. It probably hadn't intended to be a decoy, but the Americans got wind they had been rumbled and moved their radio base elsewhere, leaving a beautifully built and entirely hidden bunker unused for decades.

Until Mia intercepted the papers from Corinna. What Corinna had thought would be a matter of interest for Krister's family, had turned into Mia's lab. I hoped.

Mia had advised Corinna to block me, telling her that I was paranoid and obsessed with Johan's past. The fact I had lied to her about why I was in Stockholm hadn't helped, but when I approached her outside her office, she had already started to find Mia's insistence about me odd. She had discussed it all with her friend Linda Andersson, who added that it was Mia who had confided in her that Sanna was afraid of Johan. That had been one of the things niggling at me: Linda had posted a message of condolence to Johan, then changed her tune after Mia got to her.

I pulled out my phone. The water didn't seem to have affected it, but there was no service. I remembered that from Midsummer. Krister had had to go to a particular spot to get enough service to call the police. I had no idea where the spot was, but I'd worry about that once I had something to send.

A small animal's screech broke the silence and I jumped. I was suddenly acutely aware of how alone I was. Stillness reigned in every direction, the tranquil sea was bathed in moonlight, the woods shrouded in darkness. At least I'd easily hear someone coming, I told myself, affecting a cheer I didn't feel.

The cottage was unlocked, and the fridge was running so there must be electricity. The fridge was an antique, the rounded kind that's trendy again now, though this one was from the first time around. Sixties or so, I judged, wondering if the Americans had paid for it too.

I found a thick, crocheted blanket folded on the couch and wrapped it gratefully around myself. It took the worst off the chill of my wet clothes, though my teeth were still chattering. I was afraid to put a light on. Perched on a hill, the cottage would be a beacon in such a dark night, announcing my presence to anyone for miles around. I hesitated a few minutes, then lit a couple of candles, deciding that surely their paltry flame wouldn't pierce through the darkness.

I spread the maps and charts on the floor in the flickering light of the candles, wishing to hell I'd paid a lot more attention in geography at school. Even with the maps it was going to be next to impossible to find, I thought, hopelessness seeping through me. But I had to. If I could find it and direct the police to it, surely there would be fingerprints or DNA or *something* that would prove she had developed the drug that could stop a heart in seconds. Just because it hadn't been detected didn't mean it was magic, as Lena had pointed out. It didn't show up on standard tests simply because it didn't officially exist. Only a chemist of Mia's genius could develop something so potent without support from a state of the art facility.

'It breaks my heart she did not pursue her passion after university,' Josefin Beckmann said sadly as she showed me to the door. 'I do not understand it.'

I did. It would have been too risky for her to be associated with developing drugs, just in case any questions were ever raised over her victims. She couldn't have been entirely certain that none of the ingredients would show up in post mortem testing. Better to be one step removed just in case. Through Krister, she could keep up with his team's breakthroughs, have access to the substances he was working with, all the while making a name for herself in events and PR so that everyone forgot she had ever had an interest in chemistry.

One of Sigge Åstrand's friends mentioned seeing him dancing closely with a woman shortly before he collapsed.

Access and opportunity.

That's what it came back to, every time.

But, it was all circumstantial. She could easily wriggle out of the poison she had been spreading about Johan. The nature of gossip was that no one could be certain exactly what they heard when and from whom. There was no way to prove that Mia was the woman who danced with Sigge, or the woman Tove Svensson insisted had befriended Björne before his death. Johan and the others knew she had spent most of Sanna's final weekend locked in conversation with her, but none of them would question it.

Somehow, once I had handed it all over to the police, I would have to talk to Johan properly. Break it to him it was me that turned Mia in. The bonds between them all ran so deep, I had no idea if he would ever forgive me.

My phone beeped to life. It must be sitting in a tiny pocket of service. I swiped to open it as gingerly as I could, afraid that so much as a millimetre would cut me off from the world again. Dozens of texts and missed calls flashed up, from Johan, Maddie, Mia. I dismissed all the notifications. I'd text Maddie in a moment —

Then I saw it.

Horror washed over me as the news notification pinged up. *Woman found dead.*

Liv.

No. No —

My heart hammered, hot tears sprang into my eyes as I shook my head desperately, praying I had got it wrong. It was my fault. I had told Mia I was going to the police. I had meant to rattle her, hoped that she might panic like she did with Gustav, misstep somehow — but I never thought —

Liv. *Oh, god, Liv. I'm so sorry.* Why her?

'How could you Ellie?' Johan asked.

I looked up in shock. Johan stood in the doorway, staring at me with cold eyes.

'I loved you. There was nothing between me and Liv any more. But you killed her anyway.'

It was then I noticed the knife in his hand.

49

'Johan?'

'You killed Liv, Ellie. Why did you kill Liv?'

He was standing completely still, his voice robotic. I could barely see him in the flickering candlelight, but there was something odd about his posture. He was standing straighter than usual, but there was something chillingly childlike about it, as though he were proving he was a big boy who wasn't scared.

He didn't look like himself.

Spiders of horror scuttled down my back.

Was he drugged? Hypnotised?

Johan wouldn't hurt me, I told myself frantically. He wouldn't. Even if he believed I killed Liv.

But this wasn't Johan. I didn't know what the stranger towering over me was capable of.

He had the best part of a foot on me. He could snap me in two. I thought of the guys from the T-bana fight. Three of them. Beaten, bloody. Johan's grazed knuckles. We'd mock wrestled a few times and even in jest he could pin me in seconds, with one arm.

And now he had a knife.

'Johan, I didn't kill Liv. I've been here. I didn't even know until —'

'Why, Ellie? She wanted to be your friend.'

That weird mototonous voice sent a wave of sheer horror crashing over me. This wasn't Johan. What had she done to him?

'I'm so sorry she's dead. I honestly am. I would have liked to get to know her properly. Please Johan — just put the knife down and we can talk.'

He glanced at the knife in his hands as though surprised it was there.

Mia was standing behind him. A breeze fluttered through the cottage, casting the candlelight long and I saw glee sizzling in her eyes. Leaden terror settled in my stomach.

'Sending Johan in to do your dirty work now?' I asked.

'You're not one of my special ones,' she shrugged, her eyes never leaving Johan. 'It has to be like this.'

'It really, bloody doesn't, Mia.'

'I can't kill you. You are not weak.' She scrunched up her nose, as though this were a minor inconvenience.

'You don't know the half of it, I'm as weak as they come. Come on Mia, you and me. It would be a fair fight between us. Leave him out of it.'

Johan's fingers tightened around the knife and terror slithered down my spine.

'What have you done to him?' I whispered.

Mia turned to me then, finally, a grin of pure joy on her face. 'I told him not to be sad.'

'Why did you lie about how you met Johan and Krister?' I asked.

'What?'

'You've stolen their story. You didn't make friends with them on the first day of school. It was Krister who tied Johan's shoelaces.'

As I talked, I cast my eyes around for something, anything, I could use as a weapon, but I could barely see a bloody thing in the candlelight. The candle holders were no good, they were ceramic. Throwing one might result in a decent clunk, but I was far from confident I could hit her even at this distance. I was always last picked for netball.

Mia laughed. 'Oh did you notice that? I'm so used to telling people that I forgot Johan might have told you his version.' She shrugged. 'People's memories get mixed up, it's no big deal.'

There was one of those little stove fires in the corner behind me. Surely there would be a poker or something, but I couldn't look around to check. I couldn't take my eyes off them.

'But why? You all became friends in high school, there's nothing wrong with that.'

Could I hit Johan with a poker? My heart was pounding, stinging pins and needles of terror zipping through me. If it came to it. If it was a question of him or me?

I couldn't. I couldn't hurt him.

I'd just have to hit her, then.

'No, that's not true.' Mia shook her head. 'We were always friends. When we were small. The man in the tunnel told me Johan was my friend.'

The tunnel? Where Johan's father died? Horror clutched at my throat. She was seven years old.

I saw it then. Johan flinched. He blinked, a flash of pain crossed his face.

'Mia, go and sit down on that chair,' he said softly, in his normal voice.

She frowned at him, a flicker of uncertainty playing on her face.

'Sit down, Mia,' he repeated, more firmly.

'Johan, grab her!' I hissed urgently.

'Mia, it's going to be okay. Ellie is going to phone the police and you are —'

A flash of metal glinted in the candlelight. Johan roared with pain, his face contorted —

Blood splattered on the floor —

I scrabbled to my feet —

She had an axe.

She swung for him again —

'Mia, no —' I screamed.

Johan's shoulder was spurting blood, but he lunged for Mia even as he staggered to his knees —

I whirled around, reached blindly for the wrought iron poker set hanging by the fireplace.

Johan grabbed for the axe and Mia stumbled, righted herself, wrenched the axe from his grasp — a horrifying clunk resounded as she got the side of Johan's head, this time with the blunt edge —

He grunted as he slumped over.

I ran wildly, rugby tackled her to the floor that was slick with Johan's blood —

Wildly flailed to punch her — got her ear — her shoulder —

For fuck's sake I was shit at this.

At least I had her on the ground. I was straddling her, one of her arms pinned under my knee. She thrashed around but she couldn't quite shift my weight.

I silently thanked all those takeaways.

Johan stirred. He wasn't out cold. He was alive.

I heard the distant siren of a police boat approaching.

Oh thank fuck.

The relief weakened me, just for a second, but Mia wiggled free —

Shit —

I grabbed for her but she'd scrabbled to her feet, ran out the door —

'My boat — she'll get away —' Johan gasped.

I ran after her.

The night was still and silent, the darkness as thick as a shroud.

As I raced out into the garden, I crashed right into the motherfucking shitheaded arsewipe of a picnic table where we'd had our Midsummer dinner. Screaming in fury, I kicked the chair out my way and was rewarded by a resounding thwack to my knee.

There was no sign of Mia.

I could still hear the faint sirens, but even from the top of the hill I couldn't yet see any approaching lights.

I paused. Listening, for footsteps, the sound of the boat engine starting, any sign of her. All I could hear was the Baltic gently lapping against the rocks below.

The beach, I thought. That's where the boat must be. She would be headed there.

I put my hands out in front of me and gingerly moved forward, trying to orientate myself.

If the cottage was behind me, then the path was to my right. I started to move carefully, slowly but steadily, keeping my ears peeled for the sound of the boat.

Finally I felt the gritty sand of the path beneath my feet. I took another step and skidded, righted myself, my heart thudding. The path was narrow and steep, the rocks below it sharp.

Finally the police lights appeared in the distance, the

sharp blue glow piercing the darkness. Relief trembled through me, but they were still far away.

And Mia was near.

I could hear her breathing.

I couldn't see my hands in front of my face, but I could feel her.

I held my breath, braced myself for the poker to come flying out the darkness at me —

And then I heard something else.

A crackle. A crash.

Suddenly it wasn't dark any more.

Long flames licked the side of the cottage, the air filled with smoke.

The candles.

Johan.

A shadow caught the corner of my eye as I turned and raced back to the cottage. Mia?

I grabbed for the door handle and screamed, my hand immediately started to blister —

I kicked at the door instead and it fell open, half off its hinges already —

A billow of smoke burst through the doorway, followed by flames —

I shoved my T shirt over my head, vaguely recalling a fireman at my school telling us to cover our faces with a wet cloth. Well I didn't have any water now, this would have to do. I fell to my knees and shimmied forward on my forearms.

The floorboards were blistering, the pain in my hand and battered knee searing as I dragged myself ever forward.

Johan hadn't been far from the door. He'd collapsed just by the entrance to the little kitchen. I had to be near him —

but every time I waved my arm wildly in front of me it met only air.

'*Johaaannnnnn*' I screamed desperately, a sob of terror breaking over me.

Finally I reached out and there he was. Slumped, unconscious. A dead weight. Holy fuck how was I going to move him?

There was an almighty crash as something in the cottage collapsed. A wall, the roof, who knew, but it gave the flames a burst of energy. My eyes were watering, the heat unbearable. The fire was inches from Johan.

Grimacing against the pain from my throbbing knee, I got myself into a crouching position, somehow managed to hitch my forearms under his armpits. His T shirt was soaked through with blood, rapidly hardening in the heat of the fire, and his head lolled horribly. I gritted my teeth and pulled with all my might.

I screamed and collapsed beneath him. I'd yanked him about a foot, but it was a foot closer to the door and a blast of icy air greeted me. I could do this. Just another couple of yanks. I shuffled my bum backwards, then used my entire upper body to shift us backwards, crying out from the strain. Somehow, we moved a tiny bit more. There was another crash and a huge flame leaped forward —

With a desperate scream I shuffled again, and again, and finally we were on the porch. The grass. I had to get us to the grass. We weren't safe until we got onto the grass.

But I couldn't. Howling with terror and helplessness I tried again, but every cell in my body was drained, zinging with pain and exhaustion and fear. I buried my face in his shoulder, breathing in that familiar scent of him as I sobbed.

Then the wind splattered a gust of icy rain over us and it was the most beautiful thing I've ever felt. The porch sizzled, the fire receded to resentful embers and I felt Johan stir. The sirens were deafening and the blinding light of a police torch shone in my eyes.

Johan's hand fluttered and he shifted.

'Now you bloody wake up, you lazy sod,' I half laughed, half cried.

He reached up with his good arm and stroked my hair.

'So how do you like Sweden so far?' he murmured.

50

'They won't let us in after visiting hours,' Krister said, his eyes wide and frightened.

'Oh they will,' I grinned breezily, lacing up my trainers as best I could with one hand. My burned hand was bandaged, my knee still stiff and generally everything ached and throbbed. 'I made friends with one of the nurses yesterday, and she said she'd sneak me in if need be.'

'Why do you have to break all the rules all the time?' he asked, but there was a chuckle in his voice.

'I don't really know,' I replied honestly. 'It's kind of my thing.'

I leaned heavily on Krister's arm as we walked across Södermalm to the hospital where Johan was recovering. Where he used to work. Where he would again soon now Mia's tampering had come to light.

The first night, my nurse buddy let me spend the whole evening curled in the armchair next to Johan's bed, holding his hand as he drifted in and out of consciousness.

He had inhaled a lot of smoke, in addition to the blow to the head. They'd managed to stitch his shoulder back together, though he wouldn't be playing cricket in a hurry. His concussion was mild but the smoke damage to his heart and lungs had been touch and go, and I'd refused to leave his side, willing him to get better or I'd bloody kill him.

By the evening, he had stabilised and was sleeping when Corinna knocked on the doorframe and burst into tears. She had provided the police with copies of the maps and they had found the bunker and Mia's lab of horrors.

'I'm so sorry,' she whispered. 'It was when I read about Liv's death — I thought I had got it all wrong and I called Mia. I will never forgive myself.'

'At least you called the police as well,' I said.

'I've known her for so many years, I just couldn't quite believe —'

'Don't be too hard on yourself. I've only known her a few months and she was the last person I suspected.'

Krister had been snoozing in the other chair by Johan's bed. I glanced over with a guilty smile, remembering how I'd thought it was him until I'd remembered Mia's weird claim of tying Johan's shoelaces on their first day of school. He'd been the perfect shield for her all this time.

He had had no idea of the extent of what she was capable of, but had readily confessed the control she had held over him for years. She kept control of their finances, his phone — half the time Johan thought he was texting Krister it was Mia replying. He was terrified of her.

And nobody knew where she was. I could have sworn I saw her in the garden when the fire started but by the time the police arrived, Johan's boat was gone and so was she. A huge operation had been combing the archipelago ever since, but she seemed to have disappeared into thin air.

Sure enough, visiting hours were just ending as we finally hobbled into the hospital, but my nurse buddy rolled her eyes and let us into Johan's room anyway. He was sitting up, looking the brightest I'd seen him yet. Colour was back in his cheeks and his eyes shone as he smiled at me. I leaned over his bed and kissed him, thrilled when he responded and we snogged as Krister made puking noises behind us.

Then a roar emanated from the TV and I realised bloody football was on. Krister yelled in joy and Johan jumped. He pulled back, but held me close so I snuggled against him, feeling the warmth of his chest against my cheek as he cheered his team to victory.

THE END.

BROKEN MIRRORS (STOCKHOLM MURDERS BOOK 2)

PRE ORDER NOW!

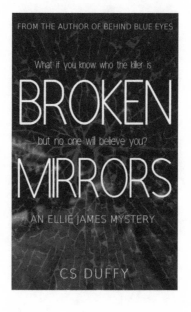

ABOUT THE AUTHOR

C.S. Duffy writes crime thrillers with a healthy dose of black humour. Her background is in film and TV, and she has several projects in development in Sweden and the UK, including the feature film *Guilty*. She is the author of *Life is Swede,* a thriller in the form of a blog - leading several readers to contact Swedish news agencies asking them why they hadn't reported the murder that features in the blog. Her supernatural audio series is currently running on Storytel in several countries and she was selected as Spotlight author at Bloody Scotland in 2018.

www.csduffywriter.com

CPSIA information can be obtained
at www.ICGtesting.com
Printed in the USA
LVHW020910170619
621442LV00003B/536